"I don't do relationships," he told her, but moved from where he stood, until he stopped only inches away from her.

"We've already had this conversation," she said and took the last step to close the distance between them. "You don't do relationships. You like your privacy. I'm focused on my career and will let nothing interfere with achieving my goals. You're attracted to me, and I'm attracted to you."

"For this one time," he said and used a finger to trace the line of her bottom lip.

Heat spread quickly throughout her body, her fingers clenching and releasing at her side as she tried to remain still for just a moment longer.

"Again," she whispered and gave in.

Coming up on the tip of her toes, Ava wrapped her arms around Gage's neck and pulled his head down so that her lips could touch his. That simple connection set off an explosion of heat that soared through her body. The memory of their night in the trailer had never dimmed in her mind; still, this touch sent her reeling with pleasure.

Dear Reader,

I've been eager to get to Gage Taylor's story because I knew he had some things to work through before finding his happy-ever-after. Ava Cannon is just what he needs, even if he doesn't know it yet!

The fun part about writing these two characters was they were so similar as far as their careers that you would have thought they'd immediately realize they were the perfect couple. But, as it is in life, things get in the way. So we're back in Temptation with more meddling folk and scandalous revelations.

Get ready for another visit to Temptation and the journey to another Taylor falling in love.

Happy reading,

ac

One
Perfect
Moment

A.C. Arthur

HHARLEQUIN® KIMANI™ ROMANCE

Recycling programs
for this product may
not exist in your area.

ISBN-13: 978-1-335-21678-6

One Perfect Moment

Copyright © 2018 by Artist Arthur

For questions and comments about the quality of this book please contact us at CustomerService@Harlequin.com.

H HARLEQUIN®

Printed in U.S.A.

™ www.Harlequin.com

A.C. Arthur is an award-winning author who lives in Baltimore, Maryland, with her husband and three children. An active imagination and a love for reading encouraged her to begin writing in high school and she hasn't stopped since.

Books by A.C. Arthur

Harlequin Kimani Romance

Winter Kisses
Desire a Donovan
Surrender to a Donovan
Decadent Dreams
Eve of Passion
One Mistletoe Wish
To Marry a Prince
Loving the Princess
Prince Ever After
One Unforgettable Kiss
One Perfect Moment

Visit the Author Profile page
at Harlequin.com for more titles.

Prologue

"Just this one time," Ava Cannon whispered as his hands cupped her butt.

"Once is enough," Gage Taylor murmured while moving them farther into her trailer.

He kicked the door closed with his foot, pausing a second to reach back and lock it. Then his hands were on her once more, his mouth crashing down over hers. The kiss took her breath away, every stroke of his tongue sending searing bolts of desire through her system until her fingers were gripping his shirt. The feel of his strong biceps through the cotton material, coupled with the hardness of his body, now pressed closely against hers, caused Ava's knees to tremble.

This was what she'd been fighting for over the last couple of months. Each day she'd stepped onto the set of *Doctor's Orders*, knowing that he would be there. The strong hands that she'd seen holding her script as he'd checked the words she'd written, monitoring them for medical accuracy, now touched her body.

"It will be enough," Ava whispered when he tore his mouth away from hers and she could take a breath.

He tugged the hem of her shirt from her pants. She lifted her arms up over her head, and he pulled the shirt off. His hands immediately went around her to the clasp of her bra, which he quickly unhooked before removing and tossing it somewhere on the trailer floor.

"Enough," he mumbled as he dipped his head. "More than enough."

His lips were on her breast then, teeth holding a turgid nipple before he sucked her in deep. Ava arched her back, her hands going to his shoulders as she tried to hold on to him. When he moved to the other breast she let her head lull back, her eyes closing to the delicious sensations rippling throughout her body.

Dr. Gage Taylor was a brilliant obstetrician and researcher. He'd come highly recommended when she'd asked who in the New York area would be a good consultant for her show. And when he arrived in her office that first day, she'd been rewarded with how jaw-dropping handsome the guy was. Ava should have known then that she was in trouble.

Now, she was pulling at his shirt until the buttons popped off. He grunted and hurried to unsnap his pants while she did the same, toed off her flats and pushed her pants and panties down her legs. His shirt was on the floor, his pants undone, his hands moving quickly to pull a condom packet from his wallet. She pushed his pants and his boxers down as he ripped the condom packet open and then smoothed the latex over his length. He wore leather loafers that he kicked off his feet before stepping out of his pants.

Ava sat on the couch. She scooted back on the wide pillows and looked up at all of the heavenly goodness that was Gage Taylor. Six feet one inch of golden honey-hued skin, ripped abs, muscled limbs and a thick, long erection. She swallowed as her gaze rested there.

"Just this once," he said, his voice deep and husky in the confined space of the trailer.

Ava licked her lips and nodded. "Yes, just this once."

He was over her by then, his lips on hers, his knee spreading her legs apart. She opened her mouth to his persistence, clasped her hands to the back of his head to hold him there. He pushed them both back to a lying position on the couch, arranging himself between her legs. He said something, but Ava couldn't hear him over the pounding of her heart and the rush of desire.

Her legs were already trembling by the time the crest of his erection touched her entrance. He pressed harder.

She moaned deeper, and their "one time" began.

Chapter 1

New York City
Three Weeks Later

Gage stepped out onto the sidewalk on a warm September morning, three weeks after they'd wrapped up shooting on *Doctor's Orders*. Despite the strange hours he'd been keeping during the seven weeks he served as an on-site consultant for the network medical drama, this morning he was expected at the hospital by nine. That meant he was taking his usual four-block walk to the Nancy Links Medical Center, where he'd worked as an obstetrician for the last four years.

He held his briefcase in one hand, cell phone in the other as he walked away from the thirty-story condo building, his Italian leather dress shoes clicking on the sidewalk. This afternoon he was seeing patients, but this morning was relatively free, he noted as he looked at his mobile calendar.

Gage had discovered early in life that being organized was a necessity. Growing up in a household with five siblings meant he had to know what was his and where his personal belongings were at all times. He'd learned a lot growing up as one of the infamous Taylor sextuplets, enough to make not repeating past mistakes one of his main priorities in life.

He looked up in time to see the light changing and then crossed the street just before his phone rang.

"Dr. Taylor," he answered because he could see from the caller ID that it was the hospital calling.

"Good morning," his assistant, Carrie, replied.

Carrie had been with him for the last six months. For his first two years at the medical center he'd been in residency, and then his inaugural research paper on infertility and the strides that had been made in the field had been published. That had propelled his career forward, and Gage became a staff obstetrician as well as a grant recipient in the following weeks to continue his research. With those dual titles, he'd been given a corner office on the hospital's fourth floor, an administrative assistant and, just recently, a lab assistant. His first admin had gone on maternity leave just weeks before his father's death last September. Since then, he'd gone through three more assistants, who had been sent to him via an employment agency.

Who would have thought that after all this time out of the spotlight, there would still be someone—actually three someones, all female—who not only knew who he was, but were also ready to claim their place in the spotlight by either working for him, or possibly sleeping with him.

Gage blamed his father's death a year ago for the renewed interest in the first African American sextuplets to be born in Temptation, Virginia, thirty years ago. After leaving his wife and seven-year-old children, Theodor Taylor had gone on to become the CEO of Taylor Manufacturing, building an empire that designed engines for a Japanese automotive company. Stock in the company had soared at the time of Theodor's death, and when it was announced that the estate would be handled by the children, Gage recalled fielding calls from newspaper reporters to investors asking about their plans for the international company. That was until Gray, the oldest Taylor sextuplet, brokered a deal to sell Taylor Manufacturing and divided the proceeds evenly among the siblings.

"Dr. Gogenheim wants to see you as soon as you get in this morning," Carrie was saying as Gage shook his head to rid himself of the memories of his father.

"Really? I didn't see anything on my calendar," he replied. "I planned to reach out to that research facility in Paris before their offices close for the day when I get in."

"I recall you mentioning that yesterday when we spoke. However, Dr. Gogenheim's assistant just called to see if you were in yet. I told her you were on your way."

"I am," Gage said just before a driver slammed on

the brakes, subsequently causing the cars behind him to do the same.

Those were the glorious sounds of a morning during rush-hour traffic. When the noise subsided, he continued. "Fine, I'll go right up to his office, but please have the number and the name of a contact person at the facility in Paris on my desk for when I return."

"Yes, sir. I'll get that information now."

"Thank you, and, Carrie?"

"Yes, sir, I hadn't gone down to get your Caffè Americano yet. I'll wait about half an hour. It will be on your desk when you finish with Dr. Gogenheim."

Gage smiled. "Thanks, Carrie."

He'd never been a morning person. To survive undergrad, med school and residency required the strongest coffee possible. Luckily for him, there was a Starbucks on the ground floor of the medical center. Gage showed his appreciation for Carrie going the extra mile to get his coffee by opening a credit account with the barista and paying them monthly for all drinks and any other items that he and Carrie ordered.

After disconnecting the call, Gage scrolled through some of the emails he'd missed in the last couple of days because he'd spent the weekend at a colleague's house in the Hamptons. He had been attending, of all things, a baby shower.

Gage approached the hospital minutes later and walked through the revolving glass doors. His honey-colored burnished leather wingtip lace-up Tom Ford shoes clicked against the polished floors as he made his way through the lobby and down the hall toward the elevators that would lead to the obstetrics and gynecology floors. He slipped his phone into his suit jacket pocket just before stepping into the elevator. When he heard someone yelling, "Hold the elevator!" he extended his arm so that his briefcase kept the door from closing.

"Thanks," the woman, dressed in light blue scrubs, said as she made her way into the compartment and pressed the floor she needed.

"No problem," Gage said and returned the smile she was so eagerly offering.

As the elevator began to move, he thought of how pretty she was, with her dark brown hair pulled back from her face and green eyes twinkling each time she looked up at him. He could ask her out, but he'd decided a long time ago that the quick, no-commitment type of interaction he preferred to have with women didn't bode well in the workplace.

The elevator stopped on her floor, and before she stepped off, she turned back to look at him. "Have a great day, Dr. Taylor."

Her arm extended, and Gage looked down at the business card she held in her hand. He immediately accepted the card and wished her a great day, as well. When the doors closed and he was alone, Gage looked down at the card, a smile ghosting his face.

"Miranda," he said and continued to read the words on the card as the elevator moved again.

She was a radiologist on the third floor. And she was hot. He tucked the card into the side of his brief-case and stepped off the elevator when it opened on his floor. He wasn't going to call her, Gage told himself.

Regardless of how good she looked. He had rules, and he had learned the hard way that it was best to stick to them, always.

"Good morning, Dr. Taylor. Dr. Gogenheim is waiting for you," the receptionist said when he stopped in front of her. "Just go on back to his office."

"Thank you," Gage replied with a nod.

He was known throughout the hospital, a fact that should have bothered him considering he despised his family's notoriety. But this was different. Gage's recognition at the hospital came primarily from being a talented doctor who brought huge research grants to the facility and added to their already stellar reputation. The Taylors of Temptation, on the other hand, had commercialized a serious health condition for thousands of couples, and topped that off with a very public betrayal of marriage vows and desertion of a family. It had been the beginning of the worst years of Gage's life.

Thankfully, that was then and this was now.

He gave a quick knock and then entered the office. Mortimer Gogenheim sat behind his desk, his thinning black hair brushed neatly to one side of his head, thick framed glasses perched on his nose.

"Good morning, Gage. Take a seat," he said.

Gage nodded and moved to sit in one of the guest chairs across from the sleek, dark wood desk. "Good morning," Gage replied. "I was surprised you wanted to see me so early. I thought the board meeting was scheduled for this morning."

Which was why he hadn't scheduled anything on his personal or business calendar. Gage wanted to be available the moment the board of directors decided he would become the youngest chief of obstetrics at the medical center. With all the research work he'd done this year, coupled with the latest grant that would fund the department's research labs for the next three years, he was a shoo-in for the position. At least that's what Mortimer had told him a couple of months ago. After that conversation, Gage was elated that his dream was about to become a reality, much sooner than he had ever anticipated.

"We had the meeting last night over dinner. My son-in-law received a job offer in Europe, so my daughter announced two weeks ago that they were moving over there. My wife was beside herself with worry at not being able to see the grandkids. So I'm stepping down sooner than I'd planned because we're going to move over there with them," Mortimer said as he sat forward, letting his arms rest on the desk.

Gage nodded. "Family first," he said. "I understand."

He did understand that concept, even if he didn't have a wife and kids of his own. Outside of his job, Gage only had his family. His five siblings—Gray, Garrek, Gemma, Genevieve "Gen" and Gia—who lived in different areas of the United States. They'd grown up in a tight-knit household, and even though distance separated them, they'd tried to remain as close as their mother always wanted.

"Good," Mortimer told him with a nod. "So I'll get right to the point."

Gage sat up straighter in the chair and thought about how his sisters were going to react when they heard the news. His oldest brother, Gray, was an overachiever himself, becoming one of the first African American billionaires to own and operate his own electronics company before he turned thirty. And Garrek was an exceptional navy pilot who was steadily moving up in the ranks. They were both tenacious and goal-oriented, just like Gage. His sisters each had stellar careers, as well. Gemma owned an upscale beauty salon in Washington, DC, while Gen ran her own software development company, and Gia worked as an executive chef at one of Chicago's swankiest restaurants.

He'd call Gemma first, he decided as he nodded and stared expectantly at Mortimer. She would never let him live it down if he didn't.

"The chief position is going to Edgar Rodenstein. He's been in this field for more than thirty years, and he's worked with the medical director before. In fact, Bart was the one who recommended Edgar for the job. So we're confident that the transition will be smooth. You, on the other hand, well, we're extremely happy with the work you've been doing in infertility and multiple birth research. We'd like you to continue in that vein, and we will possibly entertain a chief researcher position for you in the future."

Gage was stunned. The calm and relaxed feeling he'd had only moments ago as he'd stepped off the elevator had dissipated. It was now replaced with a sick feeling that had him shaking his head.

"Bart—" he began and then corrected himself "—the medical director hand-selected who would work with him?" he asked, and then answered his own question. "Of course he did."

Because that's what men like Bart Thomas did when faced with a younger, smarter and more innovative candidate. He selected the guy he knew best, the one he could control under the guise of training, no doubt. Gage was livid.

"I guess that makes sense," he continued because he had no intention of showing Mortimer how truly upset he was about this development.

Mortimer nodded and cleared his throat. "It makes perfect sense. The board agreed. The transition will begin immediately. We'll need you to be on hand in case further press conferences or other media appearances are required."

"I'm not sure that will be possible, Mortimer," he said before he could completely work through his thoughts. "These past few months have been a little hectic with my research and patient list, combined with the work on the television show. I was actually considering taking some time off."

Mortimer sat back in his burgundy leather chair, setting his elbows on the arms and clasping his hands. "Really?" he asked and arched a bushy gray-haired brow.

"Yes," Gage replied, his tone smooth and even, as if this was what he'd planned to say from the moment he walked into the office. "My brother and his wife have just welcomed twins, and I've been meaning to get down to Virginia to see them."

"Well, the arrival of babies is always a festive occasion," Mortimer said. "Especially in our business."

Gage chuckled along with him. "Definitely. So I'll be completing the proper paperwork this morning and briefing the other doctors in my department on my patient statuses."

"How long do you plan to be away?" Mortimer asked. "The department agreed to work around the shooting schedule for that show because it was good exposure for us to have your name and the hospital's name running in the credits of a nationally viewed program every week. New-patient visits at the clinic have grown by thirty percent in that time."

Gage nodded. He didn't need Mortimer to tell him that he'd been an asset to the medical center. He already knew that. Which was why being passed over for this promotion was a bunch of good-ole-boy crap that Gage did not appreciate.

"I'm aware," he replied. "Which is why I believe that a three-week vacation is not only warranted, but justified."

While Gage had adjusted his hours at the medical center during the shooting of *Doctor's Orders*, he hadn't missed a beat with his own patients and had even been on call most of the time while on set, rushing to the medical center to deliver three babies for other doctors who were on vacation. He would wait to see if Mortimer pressed this issue to play that card.

Instead Mortimer nodded, his cool gaze resting on Gage. "You're right," he said. "I'd hoped, however, that you would be available to represent the hospital to the media."

"I'd rather stay out of the media, if at all possible,

Mortimer. I'm sure you understand my reasons," Gage told him.

While he'd been more than excited to have his research paper published and enjoyed the accolades that came his way in the medical industry, Gage did not do media. He never granted interviews and did not appear for photo opportunities or press conferences. Up until this point, Mortimer had been happy to stand with his chest poked out, speaking on behalf of their department.

This was why Gage had been more than surprised when a production assistant from the television network had contacted him with regard to working on a show they were developing. He'd immediately turned them down, thinking they were asking him to star in the show. Gage never wanted to be in front of a camera again. But when he found out the position was simply as a consultant where he could lend his expertise and still stay in the background, he'd agreed.

"Yes," Mortimer replied. "I do understand."

"Well, then," Gage said as he stood. "I'll head down to congratulate Ed and then take care of the arrangements for my vacation."

Mortimer stood. "How are you going to adjust for three weeks without being at the hospital?" he asked. "You are your career, Gage."

Gage nodded because just fifteen minutes ago he'd been telling himself that, as well.

"I'm going to be with my family, Mortimer," was all he said before walking out of the office.

Gage squared his shoulders and walked as proudly as if he'd just received the best news of his life, down the hall and back to the elevator. As far as his career went, he wasn't sure what his next step was going to be, but didn't doubt that he would figure it out. He always did. For now, Gage was going to see Gray and his new nieces and nephews. He was going back to family, the only people he could ever trust and depend on.

Los Angeles

Ava wanted to scream at her mother.

It wasn't the first time, and she was fairly certain it wouldn't be the last. But instead of screaming, she used the fact that she was running late for a meeting to get off the phone with Eleanor Cannon. That was only a temporary reprieve, but Ava would take what she could get.

Coffee spilled onto the marble floor as she stepped into the hallway of the Yearling Broadcast Network. Two years ago, when Ava was just twenty-five years old, she'd walked down this same hallway with her heart pounding wildly, her entire life bound in sixty-three typed pages. The TV script for *Doctor's Orders* was the result of a year and a half's work, researching and developing her idea for the new medical drama. She was young and unknown at that time, but had landed the face-to-face meeting with Carroll Fleming through the showrunner for another show where she'd worked as a staff writer. Now Carroll was her current executive at the network after helping her to develop and launch *Doctor's Orders*.

Today's meeting was with Carroll and Jenner Reisling, a development executive at the same network. Ava was going to pitch her new series idea to them and prayed that the success of *Doctor's Orders*, currently the network's number one show on Thursday nights, would add weight to the new pilot following the lives of African American law students navigating their way through school, the professional world and, of course, love.

She was only a few minutes late but hated that just the same. Ava prided herself on being professional at all times. She'd always had to be. As a woman in the television industry, she knew she had to be on her game, no matter what her credentials were.

"I apologize for being late," she said immediately upon entering the conference room. "I know your time is valuable, so I'm ready to get started."

Carroll, with his shiny bald head and long, bushy red beard, sat forward in the chair he'd been lounging in.

"Don't speak of it," he said, pulling some papers that had been spread across the conference room table into a neat pile. "We were just talking about the ratings for the season finale of *Doctor's Orders*."

"Phenomenal," Jenner, a slim man with dirty-blond hair and dark brown-framed glasses, said. "As a first year procedural in a really competitive time slot, you knocked it out of the box with this one."

Ava beamed. That was the praise she'd wanted to hear for the last year. Actually, the last five years, since she'd decided that writing was her niche. She didn't believe it was conceited at all to like hearing that she'd done a good—no, a *great*—job with her first network show. Especially after all the critical words she received from her mother in her lifetime. If she'd listened to anything Eleanor Cannon said, Ava doubted she'd be where she was today.

"I'm elated at the show's success," she said and pulled three copies of her newest screenplay out of her bag.

The bag was huge and just a little worn around the straps. It was her favorite because it easily accommodated all the necessities she carried with her daily. Today, in addition to the script, she'd added her handheld recorder so she would be sure not to miss anything that was said in this meeting, a second spiral notebook that would be solely dedicated to this screenplay and any additional work she needed to do on it, and her newest pair of reading glasses because she'd accidentally stepped on the old pair when they'd fallen off the desk in her apartment.

"We are, too," Carroll continued and folded his hands over his stack of papers.

Jenner sat right next to him, smiling across the table at Ava.

"Yes, that's great," she continued as she pushed copies of the bound pages toward each of them. When they were both looking down at the cover page, Ava took a deep breath and let it out slowly.

"That brings me to this new pitch. Two young African American women spend their weekdays attending competing law schools, drinking and partying on weekends and navigating the murky waters of dating 24/7. This new, vibrant, urban take on sex and young professionals in the city will cater to the twenty- to thirtysomething crowd. A prime time slot would be

Sunday evenings. This would be an hour-long show, with a huge draw to advertisers geared toward the female consumer."

Jenner flipped through the pages of the script and glanced down at them. Carroll did neither. Instead, Ava found him staring at her as he drummed his fingers over his stack of papers.

"We have another idea in mind," Carroll told her.

Ava was about to open her mouth to speak, but she thought better of it. She always tried to evaluate her words carefully. Something else she'd learned from her mother, or rather because of her mother. Eleanor Cannon said whatever she wanted to say, whenever she wanted to say it. Even if it ended with hurt feelings or offense. Her mother believed that because she was a millionaire, she was entitled to speak her mind and never apologized for doing so. But Ava believed in giving people respect and demanded the same in return.

"I don't understand," she replied finally.

"Not that this wouldn't be great," Jenner began. "You've already proven that you have your finger on the pulse of what viewers want. And your pitch was quite intriguing. But I'm looking for something specific to boost our reality television programming."

"I see," Ava said. "I don't write reality TV shows."

She rarely even watched them. While they were extremely profitable and most brought in huge ratings and large sums of advertising dollars, they didn't exhibit the creativity and originality Ava liked to pour into her shows.

"You haven't yet," Carroll said, his excited smile spreading widely across his face.

The last time Ava had seen that smile was the day he'd shown up in her trailer on the set in New York to tell her they'd been renewed for a second season. That had been just six hours before she'd returned to her trailer with another man—the man who continued to creep into her thoughts on a daily basis.

"These are notes on the previous show of this kind," Carroll continued. "We want you to look at these to get a feel for the subject matter."

"You'll still have creative freedom to work this out in the way you see fit, but we're really aiming for the family reunion angle. If you can have a preliminary outline of the show in three months, we'll be ready to shoot the first pilot right after the first of the year. We already have the time slot selected. It will air at eight o'clock Thursday evening, with its debut on Thanksgiving Day. This will give us time to put a vigorous promotional plan in effect," Jenner told her.

Carroll was nodding now as he pushed that pile of papers across the table to her.

"*Doctor's Orders* is number one in the Thursday at eight slot," she said slowly, not liking where she felt like this was going.

"We know! We know," Carroll continued with glee. "That's why this is so perfect. That's why you are the perfect one to write this new script."

"I thought reality shows were supposed to be unscripted," Ava told him. "If you already have the idea and time slot locked in, you don't need me."

Besides, Marcelle, her agent, hadn't said anything to her about the network wanting her to work on a different project. She'd spoken to her late last night, and they were both pumped about the new pilot idea. Ava wasn't interested in a reality television show.

"Oh, but we do need you," Jenner said. "I believe you can bring a fresh slant to this idea and the execution of the show."

Carroll nodded enthusiastically. "We both believe you can do this, Ava. Especially since you already have a foot in the door with one of the stars of the show," Carroll continued.

"What are you talking about?" Ava asked. "This is the first I've heard of this show at all. How do I know who is starring in it?"

Carroll rubbed his thick fingers together, and Ava could swear his cool gray eyes glowed with excitement.

"His name is Gage Taylor. He just worked on *Doctor's Orders* with you," Carroll said.

Gage Taylor, as in the gorgeous doctor whom she'd spent the last two and a half months acting as if she weren't attracted to? The man whom she'd finally decided to have once and for all as a celebratory prize for the second season renewal? The guy whom she hadn't seen since that night, yet had thought about at least once each day in the past two weeks?

"He's a doctor," she said after taking a deep breath and releasing it slowly. "Is this show about doctors? Because I really don't want to work in the same area. That's why my new show idea is so different from *Doc-*

tor's Orders. One is a procedural drama, while the other will be mostly drama, with lots of sex thrown in."

"No," Jenner replied. "This show is not about doctors. It has its own fantastic and totally original idea we're trying to bring across!" Jenner told her. "It's a reality television family coming back together thirty years after their original story aired. We're going to call it *The Taylors of Temptation: Remember the Times*."

Ava sat back in her chair and stared at them.

"Thirty years ago, Olivia and Theodor Taylor had the first sextuplets born in the town of Temptation, Virginia. The parents are dead now, but we want to bring the sextuplets together again, in Temptation, to see how their lives have changed," Jenner told her. "The network is already on board with the concept and you writing it. All you have to do is grab your computer and head out to Temptation to get started."

She had never heard of *The Taylors of Temptation*. Probably because she was only twenty-seven, and this show would have originally aired before she was born. Gage Taylor had come to her via recommendation from Daniel, her production assistant, whose wife, Leslie, was one of Gage's patients. Ava had known they'd need a consultant to make sure the story lines surrounding the doctors and the clinic where they worked was as authentic as possible. So she'd taken Daniel's and Leslie's word for how good Gage was and ended up enjoying working with him. A lot.

She folded her hands in her lap and shook her head once more. "I do not write reality television," she told them again.

This time Carroll's smile disappeared, and the cold edge of those gray eyes rested solely on her.

"Then you don't write another show for this network," he said with finality.

Ava couldn't breathe. She wanted to curse or kick something…possibly Carroll. Instead she kept her lips tightly clamped.

"Look, Ava, we like you," Jenner began. "*Doctor's Orders* is doing very well, and we'd love to continue working with you. To possibly develop other shows with you in the future. But for right now, this is the show we want. Do you understand?"

She absolutely did. They were giving her an ultimatum. One Ava didn't know if she could walk away from.

Chapter 2

Temptation, Virginia

One week after the tumultuous meeting at the network, Ava drove a rented fuel-efficient car into the town of Temptation, Virginia.

For the last thirty minutes, her speed had slowed. After passing the large heart-shaped sign with "Welcome to Temptation" written in bright turquoise letters, she'd felt a bit of calm take over. The drive from the airport took a few hours, and she'd hurried at first, driving as if she was on her way to an emergency. She wanted to get this over with.

Except Ava knew it wasn't going to be that easy. She hated that Jenner and Carroll had given her no choice in this matter. Or rather, she despised that their choice meant she would either have to shop her new idea to another network—and risk news traveling that she was difficult to work with—or do what she was told to do, something she'd sworn she was beyond doing.

Ava was not difficult to work with. Not on the set of the first network series she'd written for, or as the executive producer and writer of her own show. But that didn't mean Carroll wouldn't put that rumor out there, just to keep her from working anywhere else in television. That's how the industry worked. There were lots of intimidation tactics used by those in controlling positions, and Ava was glad that hers had, thankfully, only included a delayed green light of her new show idea. She knew of too many women who had suffered in other ways.

Ava was going to write the treatment for this show. Taking the next step in her career meant that much to her. And while she was sure she could use her family's influence to work with another network or even to produce her own movie if she wanted to, Ava chose not to do that. She wanted to do this on her own merit, and she would, even if it meant approaching a family who— she'd learned from the research she'd done in the last few days—had done all that they could to stay out of the spotlight.

Mature trees ushered her along the road, standing thick and tall on both sides. The sky was a perfect blue, accompanied by the fluffiest white clouds and shimmers of golden sunlight. She'd cut off the air-conditioning and rolled down the front windows, inhaling deeply the warm, fresh air. In the rearview mirror, looking as if they were somehow following her, were the peaks of the Blue Ridge Mountains. Ava figured they were just as majestic and beautiful up close as they were from this distance.

She wished this excursion would allow time for a hiking trip along some of the famous trails she'd read about during her research of the town. But she was on a tight schedule. Jenner wanted a thirteen-episode outline by Halloween—six weeks from now—and final consent contracts signed by each of the Taylor sextuplets no later than Thanksgiving. This would keep them on schedule for shooting to begin in January. Ava tightened her grip on the steering wheel and focused her mind once more on the plan she'd come up with.

Grayson Taylor was the CEO of Taylor Electronics and had recently returned to Temptation, found a wife with twins and renovated the old Victorian house where the original Taylor family had lived thirty years ago. Just three weeks ago, Grayson and his wife, Morgan, had welcomed a second set of twins, giving them a total of four children. Ava couldn't imagine taking care of anyone but herself—four kids would definitely be out of her league. Grayson and his family would be the key to getting all the siblings on board. She'd concluded that because, as the oldest, he also seemed to be the spokesperson for the Taylor sextuplets.

She made a right turn that landed her on a dirt road and was just about to check her GPS when her phone rang. It was on the console, connected to the charger, and she pressed the button to answer without looking at the screen. She was more concerned with whether or not she'd taken a wrong turn.

"You said you were going to call me back. You didn't. I despise lies, Ava. You know that."

Ava rolled her eyes and silently chastised herself for not checking her caller ID before answering.

"Hi, Mom. I'm in the car," Ava replied because she knew her mother hated her talking on the phone while driving—even if Ava used a Bluetooth.

"Then why are you answering the phone?" Eleanor immediately asked.

Ava smiled.

"I didn't want to ignore your call. Listen, I should be at the bed-and-breakfast in about twenty minutes. I'll give you a call as soon as I get settled in."

"Bed-and-breakfast? Where are you? And who stays in a bed-and-breakfast when there are perfectly acceptable hotels throughout the world?"

Not Eleanor Cannon, that was for sure. Her mother would only stay in the best hotels, drive the fanciest cars, pay a small fortune for the most stylish clothes, and buy whatever else her inherited fortune would allow. Everything her mother did was done with style and grace, while Ava had adopted a more frugal lifestyle that drove Eleanor insane.

"I'm on a research assignment. I'll give you a call with more details once I'm settled."

Her mother would want the name of the bed-and-breakfast and a landline number to reach Ava in case cell service suddenly went down worldwide. Being an only child hadn't been easy for Ava. In the past six years since Ava's father's unexpected death Eleanor had become even more overbearing.

"That will be fine. I'll wait for your call. Drive safely," Eleanor said before disconnecting.

Ava took that to mean she'd better call her mother back, or Eleanor might send out the cavalry to look for her.

Tossing the headset onto the seat, Ava returned her attention to the GPS. The directions took her down a long cobblestoned street. Hearty mums stuffed in big black pots circled each lamppost. Cute little storefronts had twinkle lights or harvest baskets, pumpkins and gourds decorating their slice of the sidewalk. People moved about, walking slowly and staring at the decorations or what the store had advertised in their front windows, Ava couldn't tell which. What she saw on their faces, however, was, without a doubt, contentment.

She drove the remaining ten minutes until making the final turn to her destination. The Sunnydale Bed-and-Breakfast was a stately white colonial house with black shutters, nestled in the center of a cul-de-sac and surrounded by a number of beautifully mature trees. It looked like something straight out of *Leave It to Beaver* or one of those other old black-and-white family shows. Ava favored nostalgic television over today's modern reality. But while recognizing the need to grow and accept change, she still tried to bring a sense of those old-time family values and simplicity into her writing. A fact, she hated to admit, that would come in handy for this project.

She parked the car and reached over to grab her

phone and purse before stepping out. She traveled light, with only one huge duffel bag and her laptop, which she retrieved from the back seat before locking the car and heading up the brick walkway toward the house.

The bed-and-breakfast looked exactly as it had in the brochure, including the chubby shrubs lined up along the perimeter with picture-perfect precision. Ava smiled at the pair of stone bulldog statues guarding the premises as she stepped up onto the porch. Opening the door, she walked inside and was further warmed by the historic charm that continued. Scuffed wood-planked floors, and emerald-green-and-white textured wallpaper stretched throughout the front foyer and along the wall next to a winding glossy cherrywood railing.

She liked it here. Liked the ambience and was glad she'd selected this brochure from the three Saraya, her assistant, had given her. The research trip had been quickly planned once she'd decided to go through with the project. And once that decision was made, Ava had known exactly how she wanted to approach it—straight through the heart.

The Taylors had loved this town and the people who lived here. If Ava were going to write this show, she had to get to know the people here. What they liked, how they lived, what they feared, all of it. Then she'd tackle the Taylor sextuplets.

"Well, hello, ma'am. Welcome to Sunnydale," an older gentleman said.

He stood behind the front desk—a continuation of the cherrywood, with a black marble top. There was a large fresh flower arrangement toward the end of the desk, closest to the wall, along with a shiny gold bell and a placard on the other end that explained all the forms of payment accepted.

"Hello," Ava replied. "I have a reservation. My name is Ava Cannon."

The man never even looked at the computer sitting on the part of the desk that faced a bay window. Instead he stood and came around until he was directly in front of her. He extended his hand and gave a toothy grin.

"I'm Otis," he said. "Welcome to Sunnydale and to Temptation."

"Ah, thank you," Ava said and shook his hand.

He was still holding her hand seconds later when a younger man entered the lobby area.

"The paint's still wet, but the job's done, Mr. Otis. I have to head back out to Harper's place, but just let Nana Lou know we'll be sending her an invoice in the mail," the second man said.

There was a big contrast between the two men, and Ava, always one to pay attention to the details, picked up on it immediately. The first man, the older one who had just been called Mr. Otis, wore dark gray pants that were baggy on his slim frame. Black suspenders helped to keep the pants from falling down, and his short-sleeved light blue dress shirt was wrinkled, with a floral trimmed handkerchief in his breast pocket. His skin was a very weathered almond complexion, and his hair—what was left of it—was short, gray and curled close to his scalp.

The second man was much younger, probably in his early to mid-twenties. He was at least six feet tall with a short bush of brown hair, and he wore faded jeans and a plaid shirt with drops of paint all over it.

"Pardon me," the younger guy said. "I didn't mean to interrupt your check-in."

They would know instantly that she wasn't from Temptation, and it had nothing to do with the cream-colored pantsuit she was wearing. Ava had left the jacket to the suit on the back seat of the rental car so that her arms were bare in the peach tank top she wore. Her shoes were comfortable leather flats, and the flashiest piece of jewelry she wore was the diamond tennis bracelet her father had given her as an eighteenth birthday present.

No, they knew she wasn't from here because they knew everybody in this town. She could see it by the way they were assessing her.

"Hi. I'm Ava Cannon," she said and was finally able to ease her hand away from Mr. Otis's grip. She extended it to the young man, who smiled as he shook it.

"I'm Craig Presley," he said. "Welcome to Temptation."

"Thank you," Ava said. Both of them were actually very welcoming and genuine.

"No thanks necessary. In fact, since you're new to town, I would like to personally offer my services to show you around," he said.

Craig Presley had a nice smile and warm, happy eyes. He was cute and friendly, but he wasn't her type. Nor was hooking up with a guy in this town on her agenda.

"Presley? Are you any relation to a Harper Presley?"

"Yes," Craig replied. "Harper's my cousin. Are you looking to have a house renovated or built? Presley Construction can definitely take care of that for you. We're the best in town. Here, let me get you a card."

He was digging into his back pocket now, pulling out his wallet as he hunted for a card.

Mr. Otis scratched the side of his head. "If you're thinking about planting roots here in Temptation, you should talk to Fred Randall about purchasing some land or a house. Then you get in contact with Harper. She's a wisp of a pretty gal, and she's mighty talented, too," Mr. Otis stated.

"I'm just visiting," Ava said and then thought quickly of something else. "But I like what I've seen of this town so far." She shrugged. "Would be nice to maybe have a vacation home here."

Craig handed her a card. "Then Presley Construction is definitely here to work with you. Phone numbers, email and address are on the card. Harper does all the intake for new clients. I can introduce you to her. I just need to make a quick trip back to the warehouse and clean up a bit. Then I would love to take you to dinner to tell you more about Temptation."

Ava looked down at the card and nodded. Harper may be the head of Presley Construction, but she was also the fiancée of Garrek Taylor, the navy pilot. How lucky was she to have made this connection to the Taylor family so quickly?

"Or she can just take a little walk down Sycamore Lane. Three blocks past the traffic light and to the left—

you'll probably bump right into Harper at Gray Taylor's house. They're having a barbecue tonight."

And the luck just continued to flow, Ava thought with a smile.

"Oh no, I wouldn't want to intrude on a family gathering. I can just call tomorrow to schedule an appointment."

"Nonsense," Mr. Otis said. "Nana Lou baked some cookies for Jack and Lily. I told her I'd run them over there, but you can deliver them in my place. Gives you the perfect opportunity to meet up with Harper."

It certainly did. Almost too perfect, but Ava decided she would take it. This wasn't LA or New York; people here were just friendly, she reminded herself. Nobody was going to be suspicious if a stranger just showed up with a plate of cookies. At least she hoped not.

"Tell Harper I sent you to her," Craig added. "I'll take a rain check for dinner."

Ava found herself liking Craig Presley because she could definitely relate to his tenacity.

"I sure will," she said. "Thanks, Craig, and you, too, Mr. Otis."

Craig headed out, leaving Ava and Otis alone.

"Like Craig said before, no thanks necessary, ma'am," Otis replied with a shake of his head. "I'll just run out to the kitchen to get those cookies for you. Then I'll take your bags up to your room."

"That would be great," Ava told him. "Oh, wait, don't you need to swipe my credit card, get my ID or have me sign something?"

Otis chuckled. "I can get all that when you come

back. If you're thinking of getting a place here, we definitely don't want to put that off."

No, Ava did not want to put off the beginning of her second phase of research. She smiled and thanked Otis once more. She hadn't been in Temptation for more than an hour, and already she was on her way to getting this story done.

Gage had been in Temptation for two days and he was already dressed down in basketball shorts, a T-shirt and tennis shoes. Garrek's fiancée, Harper, hit the volleyball with a force Gage wasn't expecting, and he ran backward in order to save the shot. He tripped over something and fell back instead.

And then she was there.

"Hello, Dr. Taylor," she said with that smile that never failed to take his breath away.

She stared down at him, dark hair framing her pretty face, a light pink gloss on her soft lips. And Gage thought he must be dreaming.

"Ava?"

He moved quickly, coming to stand in front of her.

"I think you were trying to catch this," she said and gave a light kick to the ball he'd been after.

Gage put his foot on the ball to stop it from rolling, but did not take his eyes off her. She looked amazing, her long legs clad in cream-colored pants, the formfitting peach blouse and all that thick hair hanging past her shoulders. He'd forgotten how sexy she was.

"Yeah, thanks," he said and then asked, "What are you doing here?"

"Delivering cookies," she replied and held up a plate covered in foil.

"All the way from New York or LA or wherever you live?" he asked.

It may have seemed like an odd statement since this was the last woman he'd had sex with. In a perfect world, he would have known more about her besides her last name and professional occupation. But in Gage's world, it was the norm. He didn't need to know much about the women he slept with, because he never intended there to be anything beyond the physical. It was easier that way.

"I'm ah…on a kind of retreat," she replied. "A writing retreat."

He nodded, noting the plausibility of her response, but still wondering how, of all the places in the world, Ava Cannon would turn up in Temptation.

"And a cookie delivery service?"

She looked down at the plate and then up to him again.

"They're from someone named Nana Lou. Mr. Otis at the B and B said she promised to make them for Jack and Lily."

Gage frowned. "Who?"

He'd come to Temptation to be with his family and so hadn't met many people living in the town.

"Nana Lou is like our grandmother, but not really. She bakes the best double chocolate chip cookies ever," Lily said.

The precocious seven-year-old girl appeared, leaning against Gage's leg.

"You're hogging the ball, Uncle Gage," she continued before bending down to take the ball he still had under his foot.

"You must be Lily," Ava said, her attention shifting to the little girl Gage had been thoroughly enchanted by in the last couple of days.

He'd come back to Temptation to meet Gray's new family and had been amazed at how much he adored the children. Sure, he delivered babies for a living, and he studied ways to help every woman wishing to have a baby fulfill her dream. But Gage didn't think of becoming a father himself. Still, not even the smiling faces of youth, or the pure sweetness of babies, had been able to erase the thoughts of his one night with Ava. In fact, it had been all those things combined that kept Gage from thinking about his career situation.

"I am Lily, and this is my Uncle Gage. I have another uncle—his name's Garrek—but he's away flying planes right now."

"Oh, that sounds cool. These cookies smell amazing, Lily. Do you think I could try one?" Ava asked.

"Sure. Mommy won't let me and Jack have more than one for dessert. But Jack doesn't like to share, so you should take yours now."

"Hey, guys, Morgan is calling us in for dinner," Harper said as she joined them. "Oh. Hi," she added to Ava.

"Hello," Ava replied. "I'm Ava Cannon. I'm in town for a writing retreat and was told to deliver these cookies."

"And she's Uncle Gage's friend," Lily added.

Gage didn't know what to say. Hence the reason he'd

been standing there watching the exchange between his niece and his ex-boss-slash-one-night-stand.

"Hi, Ava. I'm Harper Presley."

"Oh, it's a pleasure to meet you, Harper. I met your cousin Craig when I was checking in to the B and B. He gave me your card."

"Really?" Harper asked. "Do you have a house that needs to be renovated?"

"No," Gage replied quickly. "She's just here to write."

Harper, with her sandy-brown hair pulled back from her face, arched a brow as she looked at him.

"You two know each other?" she asked.

Before Gage could answer, his legs almost buckled once more as a laughing seven-year-old ran into him.

"Come on, Uncle Gage, you're gonna make us lose," Jack said.

"You already lost. He fell, and the lady got the ball. That means the girls win. Right, Aunt Harper?" Lily asked.

"I'm calling interference," Gage told Jack. "We'll need a rematch."

Lily pouted, and to Gage's chagrin, Ava knelt down until she was face-to-face with his niece.

"Boys always try to cheat. I think he fell on purpose so he could ask for a rematch," she said.

A mutinous Lily nodded her agreement. "I think so, too."

Harper chuckled. "Okay, we'll have a rematch, but Morgan has dinner ready. You two run along and wash your face and hands so we can eat."

Thankful to Harper for getting rid of the children,

Gage turned his attention back to Ava. It was close to six o'clock in the evening, and the sun was beginning to set; still, the last fading rays cast Ava's creamed-coffee-toned skin in a golden hue that looked surreal. Or maybe it was because this was the first time he'd seen her outside of the sultry dreams that plagued him each night in the last few weeks.

"Why don't you join us for dinner, Ava? Gray and Morgan always cook a ton, and since you're a friend of Gage's, you should definitely be here to help us celebrate his homecoming," Harper said.

The gratitude Gage had just felt toward his soon-to-be sister-in-law dissipated as he turned from Ava to look at Harper with a frown.

"I'd love to," Ava happily replied.

"Great, Gage will bring you up to the house," Harper said. "I'll just go and tell Gray and Morgan to set another place at the table."

When Harper was about to walk away, Ava spoke again. "I really appreciate the offer. I've been traveling all day, and I don't even know if my room at the bed-and-breakfast is ready yet. I just dropped my bags off and came straight here."

Gage touched her elbow to stop her from following behind Harper.

"Why would you come here? How did you know where here was?" he asked, because no matter how his body was reacting to seeing her again, his mind was still suspicious.

Old habits were hard to break.

A breeze swept by, and Ava eased her arm from his

grasp. She pushed her blowing hair behind her ears. And Gage thought he'd never seen anyone as pretty as she was at this moment.

"Small towns are great for writing retreats. Meeting Craig at the B and B and Mr. Otis having cookies that needed to be delivered were coincidences," she said.

Gage watched her lips moving as she spoke and listened to the slightly husky timbre of her voice. Not only did he listen, but he felt as if that voice, her words, somehow touched a part of him. It was ridiculous, he knew, yet…he decided to believe her. It wasn't that big of a deal. She could go wherever she wanted without needing his permission. Just because she ended up here, at the same time he was, didn't mean anything. He needed to stop being so suspicious all the time.

"I would have never expected you to be here," he replied.

"It's work," she said. "Everything I do is about my work."

Gage could definitely relate to that. In contrast to her writing retreat, however, he had been taking the last couple of days to think about things other than his career. She was one of those things, even though he'd called himself a thousand fools for thinking about a one-time fling weeks later.

"But I can go if it's weird for you," she continued.

Was it weird for him?

Considering he hadn't expected to see her again until it was time to start shooting the second season of the show, maybe. Realizing that his body had already begun reacting to seeing her—via the beginning of an erection as his gaze dipped from her big brown eyes to the unmistakable curve of her full breasts in that tight blouse—hell no, this wasn't weird at all.

"It's cool," he replied. "But we'd better get going. From what I understand, my sister-in-law, Morgan, does everything based on a schedule these days. Something about having a set of twins in elementary school in addition to a set of newborn twins and coveting any sleep she can get."

"Two sets of twins?" Ava asked with an incredulous look on her face.

Gage nodded and smiled. He ignored the burst of pride that spread throughout his chest as he looked toward the house and the back porch, where his family had begun to assemble at the table to eat the celebratory meal. Gage never talked about his family to anyone because he liked to believe they belonged to only him. Not a part of the world, the way his father had tried to make the sextuplets.

"Yes," he continued and began walking toward the house. "My older brother Gray is married to Morgan, an elementary school teacher. They have a boy and a girl, Jack and Lily, who you just met. Ryan and Emma are the new babies. Do you like babies, Ava?"

She shrugged as she walked beside him.

"I never thought about it," she said and then looked at him with a sinfully delicious smile. "I like how babies are made, though."

The semi-erection that Gage had been trying to ignore grew instantly as he recalled her smiling up at him that night he'd moved between her legs and thrust his length deep inside of her. She'd told him how much she liked it that night, and Gage would swear that the smile she was giving him now was meant as a reminder.

"Yeah," he said grinning back at her. "So do I."

Chapter 3

"Gage was working on a television show," Gray said for the second time as they all sat around the light oak dining table on the covered back porch.

His incredulous tone was not lost on Gage, or anyone else at the table, for that matter. Gage sat back in his chair trying not to address the unspoken questions that loomed over them.

"He was a great help to the show," Ava answered. "I'm certain we wouldn't have been renewed for a second season without his expertise. Comments about the show's authenticity were constantly in the reviews."

Gage hadn't read any of the reviews for the show. He enjoyed looking over the scripts and meeting with the writers—that part made him feel useful.

"I've seen the show," Morgan said as she returned to the table.

Ryan had been fussing while they ate dinner, so Morgan excused herself the minute Jack and Lily were finished. She took the older twins into the house with her while she tended to the new baby. In the days since he'd been here, Gage had concluded that Morgan was a good mother who adored her children. She also loved his brother, almost as much as Gage suspected Gray loved her. That realization had been a shock to Gage. His brother had found love and happiness, two things Gage knew would never surface in his own life.

"I love to watch procedurals," Morgan continued once she was seated. "And I thought the idea of one being set in an OB-GYN clinic on Staten Island was a fresh take compared to most of the drama series on television these days."

"I don't watch a lot of current television shows, but Corbin Yancy also has a show on the home improvement network. He and his wife are redecorating their house in Palm Beach," Harper added.

Ava nodded. She'd just finished taking a sip from her glass of lemonade. Gage watched her small hand with the neatly trimmed nails as it slipped from the glass and rested on the table.

"Corbin is great and his wife's a sweetheart," Ava told them. "He loves the show and worked really well with Gage to make the character he played come to life on screen."

"Wow," Morgan said. "So Corbin Yancy as Dr. Steven Renfield is actually Gage Taylor, my brother-in-law. I feel like I'm related to a celebrity now."

"I'm not a celebrity," Gage quickly replied.

The comment came in a sharper tone than he'd anticipated. The questioning and concerned looks coming from Harper and Morgan irritated him. For the two days that he'd been here, Gage had been successful in simply enjoying these new members of his family, and not thinking too much about the other family members who had let him down.

"I know some things that can help make the show work, but that's all I do," he said, trying for a lighter tone this time.

"Never thought my brother would be in show business," Gray said blandly.

Gage knew what Gray was thinking. From the moment he'd walked up onto the porch and introduced Ava, he'd been sure what Gray's reaction to who she was, and how Gage knew her, was going to be. Which was precisely why, when he'd first arrived in Temptation and Gray had asked what he'd been doing with himself, Gage had left out the part where he was working on a successful television show.

"Why is that? If you don't mind my asking," Ava said.

In addition to being a very good-looking woman, Ava Cannon was candid and real. Traits Gage hadn't thought Hollywood types could have. He'd watched her on the set with the crew and the cast, and each time he'd noted how sincere she was in whatever she was saying or doing. Whether correcting something in the script, or expressing her concerns to the director, or simply accepting a meal from one of the vendors, she always made eye contact and made everyone feel as if they were on the same level. Gage had admired that about her.

"Our family doesn't have a good history in the television business," Gray answered.

"But we don't need to talk about that right now," Morgan hurried to say. "It's just so nice to have Gage here visiting, and then for you to show up, too, Ava, is wonderful. I feel like we're celebrating so much these days."

"Almost too much," Gage said quietly.

When he looked up to see that Ava was now staring at him, Gage thought it was time to shift gears.

"So, Harper, when does Garrek think he'll be back for a visit?" he asked. "It would be great to see him while I'm here."

"Not until Christmas," Harper replied.

She was a nice woman—intelligent and talented, as he'd seen by the work she'd done on the old Victorian. She was not at all the type he'd thought Garrek would settle down with, but after talking to her and meeting her family, Gage could see the appeal. In fact, he was surprised at how it made him feel that his brothers had found really nice women. The Taylors didn't believe in happy-ever-after, because that wasn't how it had worked out for their family. All the happiness they'd once known had come crumbling down, and in the aftermath, each of the sextuplets had been left to figure out not only their place in the world, but what type of life they would have as a result.

Gage opted for work and family. Seeking emotional ties with anyone else was futile and doomed to end disastrously. It was that simple.

"That's too bad," Morgan replied with a frown.

"Still, it's enough time for you to visit the hospital with me to check on the progress of the new wing," Gray reminded Gage.

Gray was working on the Taylor Generational Wing at All Saints Hospital in Temptation. He wanted Gage's input on the obstetrics and gynecology department and research program that was set up in their mother's name. Even though he'd vowed not to think about work while he was here, there was no way Gage was going to refuse to help his brother.

"Absolutely," Gage replied to Gray. He needed to meet with both his brothers, but for now, Gray would have to do.

"How long are you planning to stay, Gage?" Morgan asked. "With the holidays coming up, I was hoping to get all the Taylors to come for dinner. I know it's been a long time since all of you were together, but that needs to change."

Morgan was petite, friendly and just a little bit bossy, which Gage concluded was exactly what Gray needed in a woman.

"That's a great idea," Harper added.

"I should have a few more rooms at the house completed by Thanksgiving, so whoever doesn't stay here can come out there with Garrek and me."

"Oh, a big family Christmas sounds amazing," Ava said.

She looked at Morgan and Harper with an expression that matched the women's excitement.

Unsure what to make of that, Gage replied, "I don't know if I'll be able to get away again that soon. And I only have three weeks to stay this time."

Silence fell around him, and Gage felt uncomfortable with the thought that he was spoiling their plans. He was even more uncomfortable about Ava being here, with his family, making plans for the holidays.

"Well, I think I should be going now," Ava said and pushed her chair back from the table. "I apologize for interrupting your family celebration. But I do thank you so much for your hospitality, Morgan and Gray."

"Don't mention it," Morgan said before leaning over to nudge her husband.

"Ah, she's right. It was a pleasure having you, Ava," Gray told her.

"We're all set for our meeting tomorrow," Harper added.

Ava nodded. "That's right, we are. I'm really looking forward to hearing your ideas about tiny homes. I've been thinking about having one built for a while, just haven't had the time."

"Well, you're in Temptation now," Morgan continued. "We take life at a slower pace here than in Los Angeles. I hope you get lots of writing done while you're here. And please feel free to stop by whenever you get tired of sitting at your computer. You're welcome here anytime."

Gage tried not to frown at that statement. He'd taken Harper's offer to stay at the house she was renovating for her and Garrek.

"Thanks. I'm just going to head back now. I'll be seeing you all soon, I suppose," Ava said as she stood this time.

Gage stood, too. He didn't know why, but he did.

"I'm going to head out, as well. I'll see Ava back to the B and B," he said.

"That's an excellent idea," Morgan added with a smile.

"I'll meet you for breakfast at the hospital in the morning," Gray said.

"I'll be there," he replied.

Gage moved around the table to hug and kiss Morgan and Harper good-night. He shook Gray's hand and then went to stand beside Ava. She was looking at him with a smile, and Gage wondered what she was thinking. He wondered what she'd thought about that night after they'd been together in her trailer. And he wondered if she'd thought about him at all since that time.

That thought stuck with him as he followed her back to the B and B in his car. And when he stepped onto the sidewalk and walked with her up to the front door, he continued to tell himself that the one night of great sex had been just that—one night.

Until now.

"Come inside with me," Ava said to him.

"Sure," he replied without hesitation.

* * *

"This isn't New York," Gage said after closing and locking the door to her room.

Otis hadn't been at the front desk when they'd walked into Sunnydale. A woman with long braids and a quick smile gave Ava the key and told her where her room was located. It had only taken Ava a couple seconds to realize the woman's quick smile was directed at Gage. That, for some insane reason, turned her on.

Gage Taylor turned her on. He had since the first day she'd watched him walk onto the set. Dressed in a black suit, white shirt and purple tie, he'd stolen the breath of every other female on the set. And he wasn't even a movie star. It was his swagger, Ava later surmised. The way his slightly bowed legs moved and the expertly cut suit hung on his broad shoulders. How his goatee was cut so precisely and his skin tone resembled the most decadent caramel. The husky and confident tone of his voice and the candid and intense way he had of looking a person straight in the eye when they talked. All of that combined with his quick wit and easy humor was nothing short of perfect. Perfectly, mouth-wateringly sexy. Period.

"No," she replied and turned to face him. "This is Temptation."

It was a place she'd arrived at only hours before. She'd come here to work on a project she wasn't one hundred percent on board with. She had not come here to have sex with Gage again. But she wanted to. There was no point denying that.

He crossed his arms over his chest. The chest she'd

known, from the way his dress shirts molded to him when they were on the set, would be deliciously muscled.

"That it is," he continued, his voice lowering slightly. His gaze pinning her to where she stood.

"And I'm tempted," he said.

Ava tilted her head and once again replayed all the reasons why this was foolish. While they were currently in the off-season of *Doctor's Orders*, Gage had already signed a contract to work on the second season with her. Which made him an employee or coworker. In addition, he was one of the Taylors of Temptation, the family that her new project centered around. Her job here was to get each of the sextuplets to sign a contract that would allow cameras into their lives for three months. From her research, she had a feeling that wasn't going to be an easy feat.

So sleeping with Gage...again...wasn't a good idea.

"I am," she replied, "very tempted."

"I don't do relationships," he told her, but moved from where he stood, until he stopped only inches away from her.

"We've already had this conversation," she said and took the last step to close the distance between them. "You don't do relationships. You like your privacy. I'm focused on my career and will let nothing interfere with achieving my goals. You're attracted to me, and I'm attracted to you."

"For this one time," he said and used a finger to trace the line of her bottom lip.

Heat spread quickly throughout her body, her fingers clenching and releasing at her side as she tried to remain still for just a moment longer.

"Again," she whispered and gave in.

Coming up on the tip of her toes, Ava wrapped her arms around Gage's neck and pulled his head down so that her lips could touch his. That simple connection set off an explosion of heat that soared through her body. The memory of their night in the trailer had never dimmed in her mind; still, this touch sent her reeling in pleasure. He was a master at kissing, touching, seducing, and unlike in any other area of her life, Ava let go, let him take charge.

He slid his hand around her waist and down to grip her bottom. Ava sucked in a breath and moaned as he licked first her top and then her bottom lip. His fingers tightened on her, and in the next second he was lifting her off the floor. She wrapped her legs around him and eagerly delved back into the kiss.

"Bed," he mumbled between sucking on her tongue and gasping for air. "This time, the bed."

"Right," she replied as she realized he was carrying her to where he wanted her.

Ava couldn't think. She'd never been in this room before, so she wouldn't have been able to direct him to the bed anyway. Still, all her mind could absorb was the instant need that being near him sparked. She'd been afflicted with this situation for the past months as they'd worked closely together. And that night in her trailer, she'd perhaps foolishly thought that it would be cured. But it hadn't. She'd continued to want Gage long after that night. Only the thousands of miles that she'd put between them by returning to LA had kept her from showing up at his apartment and begging him to take her once more.

When he laid her down on the bed, Ava stared up into the face that had haunted her dreams too many times to count. He was possibly one of the most handsome men she'd ever seen. Certainly he was the best lover she'd ever had. But there was something else—she'd noticed it just now for the first time. Gage's dark brown eyes held a hint of wariness, even at this moment, a fact that shocked her.

"This is not why I came here," she said on impulse. "I didn't follow you so that we could do this again."

"Did you hear that?" he asked as he stared down at her.

"Hear what?"

"The sound of my ego deflating," he replied and then gave her that cocky grin she'd seen a few times before.

"I'm serious," she said, but found herself smiling, as well.

He shrugged and lifted the T-shirt he was wearing up and over his head. "I never pegged you for a stalker," he told her after tossing his shirt onto the floor.

She sat up on the bed and removed her shirt. "I definitely do not stalk," she said.

"But you stare," he added.

Ava's gaze snapped back to his face, as she'd been caught staring at his bare chest. He looked like he'd been sculpted instead of being a flesh-and-blood man. There was no other body like this, she was certain.

"Only when it's something I like," she admitted and kicked off the flats she'd been wearing.

Gage had removed more of his clothes during their banter, so that now he stood naked in front of her. She still had on her bra and panties, but he quickly rid her of them.

"So let's be clear," he said as he eased off the bed once more and found his wallet in the side pocket of his shorts.

"You're here to write and I'm on vacation."

Ava watched as he moved, loving the unfettered view of his butt and, when he turned toward her once more, his beautiful erection.

He handed her the condom packet and continued, "So this is just…"

She nodded as she ripped the foil and slid the latex out. "Is just one time. Right. Agreed."

Her hand moved slowly as she smoothed the condom over his thick length. She loved how he felt: hot, heavy, potent. She resisted the urge to moan, and he pushed her legs apart before coming over her on the bed.

"I'm going to enjoy this agreement," he whispered as he grinned down at her.

Biting on her bottom lip, Ava wrapped her arms around his shoulders and lifted her legs until they were around his waist. "Me, too," she said when the tip of his erection tapped her entrance, as if asking permission.

He rotated his hips. She lifted her bottom a bit off the bed until they were joined. He pushed inside her slowly. She dug her fingers into the skin of his back. He moaned until he was completely embedded inside her and her legs trembled. Tossing her head back against the bed, she gasped because there had never been a moment when she wanted anything as badly as she did right now. There'd never been another man to drive her to this point of desperation.

When he moved again it was to pull out of her slowly, and Ava thought she would scream. This was madness. It was torture. It was…intimate. It wasn't what she wanted, or rather, what she'd had in mind when she invited him up here. Her thought had been of him pounding into her with the same hungry ferocity that was roaring through her at this moment. She wanted to hear the sound of their bodies clapping together as they stroked and pushed to get to that delicious pinnacle. She did not want lovemaking because this had nothing to do with love.

As Ava had always done in her life, she took control. This way she was assured to get what she wanted. She moved quickly, catching him off guard and twisting their bodies until she came out on top. They both heaved out a breath as her hair draped down, the tips touching his cheeks as she grinned.

"I'll take it from here," she said and pushed back until she was straddled over him, his length still buried deep inside.

He gave her that smirk once more and lifted his arms so that his hands could cup her bare breasts.

"Do your thing," he replied.

And she did.

Ava rode him until they were both panting. His hands had gripped her hips, holding on to her tightly as she circled, lifted and sank down, taking everything he dished out and giving him all she had.

Minutes later, after they'd both moaned with their release, he wrapped his arms around her back, holding her against his chest. She felt his heart beating a quick rhythm, slowing only as time passed. She didn't move because she needed to catch her breath, as well. But the moment he lifted a hand and stroked the back of her head, once and then twice, as if he were enjoying the feel of her hair or something equally intimate, Ava pulled back.

"Bathroom," she whispered when he stared up at her, a quizzical look on his face.

He waited a beat before replying. "Yeah. Okay."

He released her, and Ava moved quickly, sliding off him and off the bed. "I have an early morning tomorrow," she began. "I want to get some work done before I'm scheduled to meet with Harper at her office. And I've been traveling all day so—"

He sat up, and Ava took another step back toward where she'd noticed a door, which she assumed led to the bathroom.

"Got it," he told her. "I'll get going."

"Ah, good night," she said and almost cringed at how crazy she must sound to him. *Good night. Thanks for the great sex. Now be gone.* Yes, definitely crazy.

Gage looked at her then, his gaze holding her to that spot. "A very good night, Ava."

When she couldn't decide whether he wanted her to say or do something else, or if she even wanted to say or do something else, Ave decided to cut her losses. She smiled and then turned before closing herself in the bathroom, leaving Gage—and the feeling that maybe they shouldn't have done this one more time—behind.

Chapter 4

"You're not listening."

"I am," Gage replied. He moved away from the windows where he'd been looking out at the town of Temptation.

He liked the view of thick trees, leaves already the rich orange, green and yellow of autumn and the rooftops of homes built in the colonial and Victorian style. Just beyond those homes was a field of grass that gave way to a thicker copse of trees. Farther east was the Lemil Mountain Lake, a popular tourist destination for Washington, DC, and Raleigh, North Carolina, residents, because of its less-than-five-hour drive. Feeding into the Potomac River, a tributary to the Chesapeake Bay, the lake area held fond memories for Gage.

Gray frowned before continuing. "This wing of the

hospital is dedicated to our mother. It's built to house the new obstetrics and gynecology department. As well as a spacious research facility to be dedicated to the study of—"

"Infertility and multiple births," Gage finished Gray's speech.

He turned away from the window to face his brother, who was standing a few feet away from him, dressed in black slacks, gray dress shirt and tie. Gage opted for a more casual look this morning, with jeans and a polo shirt. With one hand stuffed in his front pocket, he dragged the other down the back of his head.

"I'd like your hand in this," Gray said. "Dad wanted us to do this together."

Gage gave a wry laugh. "I'm still trying to wrap my head around you actually wanting to carry out Dad's wishes."

"We're not kids anymore, Gage," his brother told him.

Gray moved to stand closer to the alcove in the wall. Six feet tall, broad shouldered, intimidating glare—that was Grayson Taylor. He was always in control of his emotions, the situation around him, the people in his care, everything. Gray was born to be a leader. Gage, as the next youngest sextuplet, had always been carefree, fun-loving and easy to get along with. That's what Gemma would say. He wasn't the one in charge, nor was he the one the siblings thought would ever stay focused long enough to become successful. But he had, and now Gray was asking for his help. Pride swelled in Gage's chest at that thought, even though standing in this hospital talking about their father still managed to irritate him.

"I'm well aware of the fact that we're adults now. I mean, look at you with your lovely wife and four kids all settled in the house where we were born," he said.

Gray smiled. Happiness looked just as good on Gray as his expensive tailored suits.

"I love them more than I ever thought possible," Gray said.

Gage nodded.

"The way Mom loved us."

"Dad loved us, too," Gray said.

When Gage only raised a brow, Gray continued, "Look, I know about the past. We all know, Gage, we lived it. And we can't go back and change it. What we do now is what counts. It's the only thing we have control over, and it's all we have to leave our children."

"Unless you don't have children, like me," Gage countered as he fingered the keys in his pocket.

Touching that one key in particular had his mind circling back to the day he'd found out he didn't get the promotion. As disappointed as he'd been, Gage stayed at work that day. But instead of making the call to the foundation in Paris, he spent the day preparing for his time off. He drafted memos for Carrie to send to the other doctors in his department with notes about his patients with specific health concerns and tests that could not be rescheduled, and at the end of the day he returned to his apartment to pack for his trip.

The envelope that Gray had sent earlier this year was still unopened, sitting on the edge of Gage's desk in his home office. After their father's death, Gray had found envelopes marked for each of the sextuplets and a bank account under the name of Taylors of Temptation LLC. Each of the siblings were named as owners of the account holding a balance of 6.8 million dollars. In death, Theodor Taylor had been more than generous with the children he'd left for a production assistant all those years ago.

For endless moments Gage had simply stared at the envelope, knowing that now was the time. When he'd first received the envelope, he'd wanted to ignore it and whatever was inside of it, because it had come from his father. But since he was planning a return to his childhood home, Gage figured the time for ignoring the envelope had passed.

There were six sonogram pictures inside. They were lettered, so Gage put them in order from A to F. He was "Taylor Baby E" and he stared at that picture for some time before moving on to the only photograph from the envelope. It was of Theodor and Olivia holding their six little babies while sitting on the couch in the old Victorian house like one big happy family. On a ragged sigh, Gage had set all the pictures aside and checked the envelope one last time before tossing it into the trash. There was a key inside.

"Hey, you still with me?" Gray asked, interrupting Gage's memory.

Gage cleared his throat and pulled his hand out of his pocket.

"Ah, yeah. I'm good," Gage said. "It's cool. I'm on board. Do you have a plan for this wing? I mean, something in writing I can review and then add to if necessary?"

For a few seconds Gray just stared at Gage, then he took a few steps, his dress shoes quiet on the beige carpet.

"I do. They're in my home office. Is everything all right, Gage?"

"Of course everything's all right. Why would you ask me that?"

"Oh, because about five months ago Garrek suddenly appeared in town under the pretense of just stopping by for a visit. Turns out he had been reported as AWOL and needed an attorney to get his military career straight. So I'm asking you again, is everything all right?"

Gage had heard—via Gemma—of Garrek's troubles in the navy, and he'd reached out to his brother about six weeks ago to make sure that he was doing well in his new position.

"I should have come for a visit sooner," he told Gray. "I just didn't have time, or I didn't make time, if I listen to what Gemma has to say. I didn't get a promotion I was looking forward to at work, so I figured now was as good a time as any to take a step back and reevaluate things. And I opened that envelope you sent me."

Now Gray nodded. He folded his arms over his chest.

"What was in it?" Gray asked.

Gage shrugged. "Just some sonogram pictures of us and a picture of Mom and Dad."

"Speaking of that, we haven't had any success in figuring out who transferred that money into the Grand Cayman accounts."

"Garrek said they'd come from an address here in Temptation," Gage said.

"They did. But the house was used as a rehabilitation center at that time. There were at least twelve adults living there during the month the deposits were made."

Gage shook his head. "Is it really that important that we find out who put the money into those accounts? I mean, Dad is gone and whoever made the deposits is likely gone, too, so why shouldn't we just move on?"

"You don't want to know?"

"I don't want to live in the past," Gage told him. "My whole purpose in being here right now is to look forward to the future."

It had taken Gage a long time to be able to say that. He only wished that he totally meant it.

"And Ava Cannon is your future?"

Gage immediately tensed. He inhaled slowly, determined to keep his body and expressions as normal as possible.

"Ava Cannon is a television producer and writer. I have a professional relationship with her."

When Gray tossed his head back and laughed, Gage frowned.

His brother clapped a hand on his shoulder and said, "You keep telling yourself that."

Gage didn't reply to that comment because he hadn't come here to talk about Ava.

"Why don't you just tell me more about this facility?" he said instead.

And when Gray kindly obliged, Gage walked through the hallways of the hospital, listening to his brother talk about the town, the doctors and the additions he had made. He did not think about the vixen who had once again brought his body to a fierce release last night.

Or the fact that despite their declarations to the contrary, and what he knew he should do, Gage wanted her again.

Ava finished the last bite of the best meat lover's omelet she'd ever had while scrolling through pictures of tiny houses on her iPad.

"Presley Construction has never built a tiny house," Harper said from across the table where they sat in Ms. Pearl's Diner. "But one of my new interns is fascinated by them and has shown me some drafts she made of a couple. If you're really interested, I can set up a time for us to meet with Fred Randall. He's the best real estate agent in town. Actually, he's the only agent in town," she added with a chuckle.

Ava looked up as she reached for a napkin. Wiping her mouth, she chuckled, as well.

"Small town, I get it," she said. "I don't know if I'm ready for that step just yet. I only wanted to get your thoughts about the idea."

That was partially true. Looking at tiny houses had become one of Ava's guilty pleasures in the last couple of years. With work and warding off the blind dates her mother routinely sent her way occupying most of her time, there was rarely time to do the things she loved.

Harper sat back against the red vinyl-covered booth. Her sandy-brown hair was pulled back, hanging down in a straight ponytail. She had inquisitive brown eyes and a pretty freckled face.

"Are you sure you want to build a tiny house in Temptation? I mean, you're a producer and a writer. Why would you want to live here as opposed to in some luxury condo or mansion in LA?" Harper asked.

"I have a condo in LA. My mother is only twenty minutes away and drops by whenever she feels like it. My agent also drops by a lot instead of calling to discuss whatever business she has with me. So sometimes the condo can be a little too busy for writing. I'm always looking for a quiet place to get work done."

Harper chewed the last piece of her blueberry muffin. "I see. So this would be like a vacation home?"

"Something like that," Ava replied. "Your family has lived here for years, correct? Did the Presleys always know the Taylors?"

Ava had been up all night thinking of how she would start the conversation with Harper. She'd also been thinking about Gage and how they'd ended up in each other's arms once more. The last thought had given her much more trouble than the first.

"My father knew Theodor Taylor pretty well, and my grandfather knew Olivia Taylor's family. They both said the two seemed to be revitalized by the birth of the sextuplets. And there are people around here who still talk about having television crews here all the time, boosting revenue for local shops and B and Bs that housed them. It was a pretty exciting time."

"And now? I mean, in the years since they've been

gone, it seems like the town is still bustling without the added attention," Ava stated.

"You're right." Harper finished off her glass of water with lemon. "The town has come a long way and we've thrived over the years. But I have to admit that when Gray came back last year and saved the hospital and community center from going into a stranger's hands, the people here were relieved. It's like they've always wanted a Taylor to live here again."

Ava smiled as she digested that tidbit of hopeful information. "I'm sure you're happy they came back. Especially Garrek."

Harper's smile was quick and brilliant. It touched every part of her face from the rise of her high cheekbones to the little light that appeared in her eyes.

"I wasn't looking for love," she told Ava. "I was just trying to do a good job for Gray and Morgan, and then he appeared. It's been a roller-coaster ride, believe me, but one I'd take over and over again."

Ava tilted her head and resisted the urge to say, "Awww." She wasn't a romantic—far from it, if truth be told. Grand gestures like candlelit dinners, flowers and frilly words didn't mean much to her. Maybe because her parents didn't have that type of relationship. Or it could be that she'd watched too many girls in high school and college falling for one guy after another who gave them the words, the gestures, even the gifts, only to have the relationship ultimately break apart in the end. Either way, Ava had known all along that happy-ever-after was not for her. Tops on her agenda was professional success. After that, well, she'd settle at some point with a happy-for-now ending.

"I wish I could have met him," she said instead. "Gray seems like a nice man. He's definitely devoted to Morgan and the children."

"Oh, there's no doubt about that. They all have his heart and soul completely. I love being with them at the house because that love just radiates throughout the walls. And I'm glad that Gray's move back here seems to be bringing the other siblings back to Temptation one by one."

"Really? Do you expect the sisters to return to town soon?" Ava asked.

That would be perfect for her.

Harper had just begun to shake her head when her gaze drifted over Ava's shoulder and her smile spread once more.

"I'm not sure," she said. "Morgan's definitely trying for that big Christmas gathering. But for now, I think the whole town is just curious about his return," Harper said.

Before Ava could ask who she was referring to, or even turn to look in the direction of Harper's gaze, he was there. Standing at the table, staring down at them with dark brown eyes and that sexy-as-hell smile.

"Good morning, ladies," Gage said.

"Good morning," Harper said. "I thought you and Gray were having breakfast at the hospital this morning."

"We were," he answered. "But trust me, I've had

enough hospital cafeteria food. Thought I'd try to find some real sustenance here."

Harper and Ava both chuckled.

"Well, Ms. Pearl makes the best waffles. I can't eat them on mornings when I have to work because I get so full and they put me right to sleep. But you should definitely try them."

Gage was nodding his agreement when Harper began to stand.

"I have to get going to another site now, but, Ava, if you want to continue talking about the tiny house, just give me a call."

"I will," Ava answered while ignoring the questioning rise of Gage's brow. "Thanks so much for taking the time to talk to me about it."

"No problem. I'd love to work with you on the project. Just keep me posted. And, you, I guess I'll see around," Harper said to Gage. "Maybe tonight at the wine festival?"

"There's a wine festival tonight?" Ava asked.

Harper smiled as she moved out of the booth and Gage took her seat. "There's always a festival or celebration or some type of event going on in Temptation. We're heading into our fall festivities now. So tonight's the wine festival, and then in a few weeks we'll have the fall festival and pumpkin-carving contest. After that we're full swing into the holidays, and believe me you haven't seen anything until you've seen Temptation all lit up and ready to celebrate Thanksgiving and Christmas."

Again, Ava wanted to sigh with contentment. She'd

never lived in a small town and so had never experienced festivals or pumpkin-carving contests. Her childhood had consisted of boarding schools, summer camps, etiquette classes, ballet lessons and formal dinner parties.

"Well, I love wine, so I'm definitely there," she immediately replied.

"Then I guess I'm going, too," Gage said cheerfully.

"Great!" Harper said, excitement clear in her voice. "See you both later."

It was that excitement that put Ava on edge. Who was she kidding? Gage was putting her on edge. Again.

"So you love wine," Gage said immediately when they were alone.

Ava was saved from providing an answer when the waitress came over to ask what he wanted. He ordered the waffles and orange juice, and Ava thought the woman's face might actually crack, she was grinning at him so broadly. She shook her head at the obvious infatuation and wondered if Gage dealt with this all the time. And if he liked it.

"I need to get back to my writing," she said, suddenly irritated.

Gage reached a hand out quickly to touch her wrist. "Keep me company while I have breakfast," he said. "Otherwise that waitress is going to keep coming back, and I'm really not in the mood for that type of attention right now."

"So that not-so-subtle flirtation happens to you all the time?"

He shrugged. "Sometimes."

"And you normally like it, but not today. I see. Well, what makes today so different?"

Damn. She sounded testy and hated it.

Gage sat back, resting his hands in his lap now. "I don't know what's different," he told her. "I'm still trying to figure it out. But, maybe it's you."

No. It couldn't be her.

"That's ridiculous. We're not committed to each other in any way," she stated. But inside she wondered if that should actually be a question.

The thought was totally foolish. This was Gage Taylor, an employee and the subject of her new project.

"No. We're not," he told her. "But we are sleeping together."

"It was just for one ni—" she started to say.

Gage arched a brow again as her lips snapped shut.

"Look, I'm not in the market for a relationship any more than you are. But I like honesty. So I try to be as honest with myself as possible."

Ava tried to ignore the sting she felt when he said "honesty."

When he continued, she took a sip from her glass.

"We've been together twice now. That doesn't make us a couple, but it certainly classifies us as sleeping together."

She couldn't argue the logic.

He nodded and thanked the waitress when his food and juice were delivered.

The offer to get him anything he wanted and yet another bright smile had Ava's fingers fisting at her sides.

She forced herself to breathe and relax because she was being ridiculous.

"Well, I can work while you eat," she said and then looked down to her iPad once more.

"Or you can tell me why you're talking about building a house here in Temptation if you just came for a writing retreat," he said.

Right, Ava thought as she took another drink from her glass. She could tell Gage why she was lying about her real reason for being here. That was sure to go over well.

Chapter 5

"I'm still waiting for a call back on that rain check."

Ava turned at the statement and found herself staring up at Craig Presley.

It was a little after seven in the evening, and since daylight saving time hadn't occurred yet, the sun was just waning in preparation to set. The Fall Wine Festival was being held at Treetop Park, which was just down the street from Temptation's town hall.

After spending her day walking around the town and talking to the wide array of citizens, Ava had headed back to the B and B, where she'd showered, checked emails and dressed for the festival. When she'd stepped outside again, it was to learn that the evening weather had shifted to a more comfortable temperature than earlier, so her decision to wear the navy blue ankle pants and beige sleeveless blouse with nude-colored sandals was a smart one. She'd driven the fuel-efficient hybrid rental car and parked on the street across from the park. The one with all the colorful houses.

"Oh, hi, Craig. I'm sorry. I've just been busy writing and stuff."

He smiled, a really nice smile. Craig was a good-looking guy who probably had women smiling at him the same way Gage did. She shook her head in an attempt to get Gage out of her mind.

"It's cool," he said. "I understand. We just finished up a big project, so I'm glad to have the festival to unwind a little."

"It looks like a good crowd," she said turning her attention toward the stalls and tents where people were lined up.

"Come on, let's start tasting," Craig told her and took her hand before she could respond.

They walked past two stalls with super long lines and when Craig joked about people in Temptation not being afraid to get drunk in public, Ava laughed.

"What's so funny?" a woman who had just stepped in front of them asked.

She wore gray dress pants with a purple blouse. Her hair was feathered back from her carefully made-up face, and her lips pursed as her eyes assessed every part of Ava.

"Hi, Ms. Millie," Craig said, gripping Ava's hand a little tighter.

"Craig," the woman—Millie—replied. "You have

manners, son, I know your daddy taught them to you. So make the introductions."

Rude didn't quite seem to describe this woman.

"I'm Ava Cannon," she said because she was a grown woman and did not need Craig to make introductions for her. "I'm visiting Temptation on a writing retreat."

She was losing track of how many times she told that lie, but didn't want to think about that at the moment.

"Ava Cannon," Millie said and continued to look as if Ava had body odor or food stuck in her teeth.

"I'm Millie Randall. Chairperson of the chamber of commerce. We usually like to welcome the visitors to Temptation personally. But I didn't know you were here. Not until this morning at least when I saw you coming out of the diner with Gage Taylor."

"Yes. I had a breakfast meeting with Harper this morning, and then Gage showed up." For whatever reason, Ava felt like she needed to explain.

"And now you're here with Craig. Well, it seems you're certainly getting around. Are you writing about the men of Temptation?" Millie asked.

"I hope not," Gage said from behind Ava.

Her heart skipped a beat at the sound of his voice, but she did not turn to look at him. This situation had gone from strange to uncomfortable in record time.

"Hey, Gage," Craig said. "Glad you could make it to your first wine festival in Temptation."

Gage had come to stand next to Millie, across from Craig and Ava.

"I thought Ava and I would enjoy our first festival together," Gage said.

"Hmmmm." Millie made the sound and looked skeptically from Gage to Ava, letting her gaze linger there.

Ava wanted to scream. Or turn and run back to her car and drive all the way back to LA. Anything to not be in the middle of something she didn't even understand herself.

This was silly. She wasn't doing anything wrong. Gage had said so himself—they weren't a couple.

"I just got here and ran into Craig," she said.

"And then we ran into Ms. Millie," Craig said.

Millie nodded. "And now we're all here together."

Ava remained silent.

"Why don't you come with me, Craig? I have something in my car for your father. You can take it to him."

Craig looked at Ava.

"She'll be fine with me," Gage said in a stiff voice.

"Come, Craig," Millie commanded and turned around to start walking away.

With an audible sigh, Craig released Ava's hand. "I'll be back," he said to her.

"Oh, don't worry about it," she told him. "I'll probably leave in a few minutes anyway. I still have work to do."

He gave her a quick smile as he back-walked in the direction Millie was heading. "That's fine, but my rain check still holds."

Ava smiled. "No problem."

But there was a problem. When they were alone, Ava felt it. She couldn't explain it, but she felt it in the way Gage was staring at her.

"So," she said finally because she was tired of standing there feeling ridiculous. "I'm going to just grab one drink, and then I'll be going."

He wasn't frowning, but he didn't look happy either. "I think we both need a drink."

That was an understatement, and the first booth they made it to, Ava eagerly accepted one of the red wines they were offering. It went down smooth and had a sweet taste, so she took another. She didn't know if Gage was trying the white or the red wine, but she finished her second and was just swallowing the third, when he stopped her.

"Slow down there. You have to pace yourself when you come to these things. Otherwise I'll have to carry you back to the B and B."

Gage's voice was deep, and rubbed against all of her nerve endings with quick and potent efficiency. The fact that she was still undeniably attracted to him after their two hookups was not nearly as surprising as the low hum of guilt she'd been carrying with her since answering his question about her tiny house quest this morning.

"Oh, no worries about that," she replied. "I can hold my liquor."

"Really? Spending your evenings in bars putting back a few is how you roll?"

His tone was lighter than just moments ago, but Ava didn't feel like laughing.

She shrugged. "Boarding school wasn't nearly as prim and proper as my mother thought it would be."

He nodded. "So you were that girl, huh? Boarding schools, fancy cars, Ivy League college."

"You attended Columbia for undergrad and medical school," she said.

"Checked up on me, did you?"

"I did my research," she said. "As I do with all the people I work with."

"That makes sense," he replied.

He took the empty glass from her, their fingers brushing with the action. She was just about to pull her hand away when Gage reached for it.

"I'm not a holding-hand type of guy," he said, staring down at her fingers.

Ava was about to say that she wasn't either, but that would have been silly since Craig had been holding her hand when Gage joined them.

After a few seconds more, he released her hand and returned her cup to the stall.

Okay, she was being foolish, there was no reason this should feel awkward. She wasn't committed to Gage, and she hadn't been doing anything wrong with Craig.

So when Gage turned to her again she started to walk, and he joined her.

"I know this is your first wine tasting in Temptation, but have you been to one of these before?" she asked after they'd passed a few stalls decorated with plastic vines and grapes.

"I've been to wine and cheese receptions in the city, and I have a friend who lives in the Hamptons who has an annual get-together to showcase his family's vineyard, but this is different."

"I agree," Ava replied. "This is different."

He may have thought she was referring to the wine

festival, but she wasn't. Her thoughts were circling more around the fact that she was actually thinking about everything she'd said to Gage in the last two days, versus the two times they'd spent in each other's arms, and the truth of why she was here. It was complicated, and while she could simply tell him everything right here and right now, she didn't.

What Ava did do, however—and to her utter embarrassment—was trip over some power cords that had been stretched across the grass from one booth to another. With her arms flailing forward, she prayed she wouldn't fall flat on her face, but her feet were already doing some type of clumsy dance that almost assured that fate.

"Whoa, there," Gage said.

His arms went around her waist, and pulled her back against him as his words whispered into her ear.

A few choice curse words and a deep breath later, Ava's feet were once again solidly on the ground while her cheeks fused with heat. "These cords should probably be stretched behind the tents. Instead of across the path where people have to walk."

"That's very true," Gage replied.

His lips were close to her ear so that his words were warm and…oddly sexy. The arm he still had wrapped around her waist felt almost possessive, and her blouse rode up her back at their close proximity.

"I'm okay now," Ava said nervously and attempted to move out of his grasp. But he held on.

"You sure? How many glasses of wine did you have before I showed up?" he asked with a chuckle.

Ava managed a smile even though she was beginning to feel pretty warm in the cool autumn evening air.

"I'm not drunk, Gage. Just a little clumsy, I guess."

Even though she'd never been known to be clumsy before. Nor had she considered herself easily flustered by some guy.

Pulling down her shirt, she looked at Gage and tried to keep her smile in place. "The cords are a hazard and could incite a lawsuit."

"Say that a little louder, and I'm sure by night's end, everyone in town will fall over themselves trying to make your visit here as safe and enjoyable as possible. That's how threats tend to work here," Gage said.

"I didn't," she replied. "I mean, I wouldn't. I was just saying that someone else might. And how do you even know how people here would act? This is your first time back in Temptation since you were a kid."

For a few seconds Gage looked at her oddly, like maybe she shouldn't know that about him. Or maybe he just didn't like hearing that little bit of truth.

"And besides, different people have different reactions," she said after clearing her throat.

They were standing in the middle of the walking path and a woman bumped into Ava, mumbling a quick "excuse me" as she moved to another booth.

"Let's get out of the way," Gage said, touching her elbow.

They walked past the row of tents to an open area where lawn chairs and blankets were spread out around the gazebo.

"Morgan and Gray are trying to get a babysitter so

they can come out tonight. So I was sent down here early with blankets and instructions to get a good spot facing the stage."

"I didn't know there would be music," Ava said and turned to look at the men setting up instruments in the large gazebo.

This was a perfect location to view a concert. There were two large screens set up on either side of the gazebo for those in the back to see.

"Yeah, I hear they do this twice a year," he told her. "Have a seat."

Ava looked at Gage and then down to the blankets before taking him up on his offer and sitting down. He followed, but he leaned back so that he was propped up on one elbow right beside her. If she lowered her hand, she could touch the small mole just beneath his right eye.

She didn't, of course. That would have been... intimate.

"I don't remember anything like this when I lived here. I was only seven when we left, so most of my memories consist of riding bikes up and down our street and going to the lake for picnics," he said abruptly.

Ava waited a beat before following his lead.

"Did you like living here?" she asked.

He reached out and touched the tips of the belt knotted at her waist.

"It was a house in a town," he replied. "At the time, I didn't know anything else."

"But it must have been fun in that big house, and being celebrities." The last word was spoken quietly.

His fingers paused on the material as he slowly looked up at her.

"It wasn't a choice," he said. "We never had a choice in the matter."

This time they would, Ava thought. She would lay it all out for them, and she would offer them the opportunity to say what they would like their show to be.

"I know a few child stars, and they're ecstatic about being on television. Mostly they're happy when the workday is over for them and they can play with whatever new and not-yet-on-the-market toy their agent has acquired for them."

She chuckled lightly, but Gage did not crack a smile.

"When you build your tiny house, you should look for a space like this," he said after a brief pause. "A wide-open area with a killer view."

So they were back to her lie...or rather, her omission.

"A view of a stage?" she asked jokingly.

"No," he replied with a shake of his head. "Look beyond the stage, Ava. Look at what nature has for you."

She did as he said. She shouldn't have. The moment she saw the mountaintops pressing into the fading purple and blush sky, she sighed and silently agreed. This was a view she could wake up to each morning. If she were actually moving to Temptation.

"It's a great view," she said. "Do you recall waking up to it when you lived here?"

"As I said before, I left when I was seven," he replied. "My mother packed us up and moved us to Florida. We lived in a house on Pensacola Bay, so my view there was of the water. I've loved the water ever since."

"I don't know how to swim," she said absently. "I grew up in Beverly Hills. We had a pool, but I never learned how to swim."

It sounded strange. Everybody knew how to swim. Right? It wasn't her fault that she had piano lessons during summer camp when other children were swimming in lakes and sleeping in tents. And when her parents had pool parties, Ava wasn't invited. When her parents weren't having a pool party, the pool was gated off because Eleanor didn't want Ava to fall in and drown, since she didn't know how to swim.

"I can teach you," Gage stated evenly.

"What?"

"I can teach you how to swim," he repeated.

Ava looked down at him again, just as the music began. More people had joined them on the grass, some standing, others sitting on their own blankets. Gage pushed himself up to a sitting position and scooted closer to her. After the first few melodic strands were played by the jazz quartet, she replied, "I'd like that."

She'd always wanted to learn how to swim, and what better way to learn than in Gage Taylor's arms?

Gage had reserved the indoor pool at the community center for a few hours. He was going to teach Ava how to swim. And that was all. He could do that.

What he couldn't seem to do, to his dismay, was forget how he'd felt seeing her holding hands with Craig Presley. It didn't matter. Gage had spent the last two days telling himself that. Ava Cannon was not his to feel possessive over. Yet, he'd wanted to snatch her hand away from Craig's that night. He'd wanted to let Craig and any other guy in this town know that she was with him. But she wasn't, at least not in that way.

She was, however, walking toward him wearing a simple yellow bikini that looked like sunshine against her golden brown skin, beneath a sheer white shirt that brushed over her knees. Her hair was piled atop her head in a way that reminded him of how she looked in the moments after they'd both reached their climax. Her face was free of makeup and as lovely as he'd ever seen it.

"Hi," she said when they were standing just a few feet away from each other.

"Hi yourself," he said over a tongue that had grown thick with lust. "Glad you could join me."

Gage was lounging in the hot tub while he'd waited for her to arrive. The way his body instantly reacted to seeing her made him grateful for the warm rolling bubbles around him.

"Are we swimming or soaking?" she asked after a few seconds of silence.

"Swimming, of course." He resisted the urge to frown as he turned his back to her and walked up the three steps to exit the hot tub. His black swim trunks were baggy enough—he hoped—so that when he turned to face her, he didn't embarrass himself and possibly her at the same time.

"I did tell you that I've never had a swim lesson before," she was saying as she moved to one of the lounge chairs and dropped the large bag she'd been carrying. "Right?"

"You did. So we'll take this slow."

But the moment she grabbed the hem of that shirt and pulled it up over her head, all thoughts of slow vanished from his mind. He wanted to take her, hard and fast, right there on the lounge chair, or in the pool.

"Great," she said as she turned to him. "I appreciate you taking the time to do this."

Yeah, he was doing a great deed here. Teaching her how to swim. And thinking of how quickly he could get her out of that skimpy bikini and on top of him.

"It's no problem. Everyone should know how to swim."

Gage cleared his throat and mentally kicked himself for being a horny cad. She was serious about learning, so he needed to get serious about teaching. Which would probably involve touching.

With a shake of his head, he led them to the side of the pool that was five feet deep.

"Come on in," he told her after stepping into the chilly water. He immediately bent his knees so that he was submerged up to his neck, acclimating himself to the new temperature.

"Oh!" she said with a shiver after sitting on the side of the pool and putting her feet in first. "Cold."

"Yeah," he replied with a nod and a smile.

Gage walked over to where she sat, touching her ankles and then smoothing his hands up and down her legs, introducing the cold water to her skin.

"You have beautiful eyes," he said while his hands continued to move. "That's one of the first things I noticed about you."

"They're just brown," she said and tilted her head while staring at him.

"They're expressive," he replied. "Whatever you don't say with words is mirrored in your eyes."

She looked away, and Gage moved in closer until his shoulders were between her knees. He moved a hand from her leg and cupped her cheek, turning her gently until she faced him again.

"That's how I knew you wanted the same thing I did. In the studio, each time we looked at each other, I knew," he said, his voice gruff with growing arousal, and just a hint of something more.

"There's a professional code of conduct," she replied before her tongue snaked out to lick her bottom lip quickly. "I like to follow my own rules. Especially on set. And sleeping with my consultant wasn't a good idea."

His hand slipped down to the smooth column of her neck. "The idea may not have been good, at first," he said. "But damn if we weren't great together, Ava. Both times."

Gage watched as she tried to deny it. She opened her mouth, snapped her lips closed and thought about what to say. But her eyes were already telling him—and his body—what he wanted to know.

"I don't know how to explain it either," he said. "I'm not usually so taken by one woman."

She nodded. "Right. You're like the rolling stone," she said.

Gage froze, the lyrics to The Temptations' famous song playing in his mind. "No. That was my father."

"I—" Ava began, but Gage touched a finger to her lips.

"I can't think of anyone but you. Since the first day on set, it's been you in my mind day and night. I've given up trying to explain it," he told her.

In fact, he'd decided that maybe it was best not to overanalyze this. They were attracted to each other, and that was that.

"Besides," he said, bringing his other arm up to wrap around her waist, pulling her closer to the edge of the pool, "we're not technically working together right now. The second season doesn't start taping until next year."

The slight tilt of her lips had his chest tightening.

"You've thought of everything, haven't you?"

"No," Gage said. "I've only thought of you, Ava. Only you."

In the next instant Gage was pulling her into the water with him, wrapping her legs around his waist as his lips met hers. Her arms were twined around his neck, and their tongues joined together in a delicious duel.

That tightening in Gage's chest simmered to a warm glow that spread throughout his body, even as they stood in the cold pool water. Her breasts pressed into his bare chest as she licked hungrily over his lips. His fingers splayed over her back before moving down to grip the plump globes of her bottom. She tightened her legs around him, pressing her center into him. Gage groaned with the deep pangs of sexual hunger that pierced through him.

He moved his fingers down farther, beneath the rim

of her bikini bottom until he could feel the crease of her backside. *Farther*, Gage thought. He needed to go farther, to touch more, to feel… The second he pushed through the warm folds of her center, the pounding of his heart grew louder, echoing in his ears.

Ava arched her back, her hands moving to his shoulders, blunt-tipped nails digging into his skin. Through partially opened eyes, Gage watched as passion played over the delicate features of her face with his touch. Tracing his fingers back and forth through her arousal-coated folds had her eyes closing, lips parting as she moaned.

She felt like heaven, like the finest silk beneath his fingers. When she whispered his name and Gage pressed one finger deep inside her entrance, Ava bucked over him, and Gage eased in another finger. Her hips began to move, pumping against his fingers as he thrust them in and out of her. Water sloshed around them, creating a cool reprieve from the fiery passion rolling over them at this moment. She pulled her bottom lip between her teeth, in a look that was as enticing as any *Playboy* centerfold Gage had ever seen. Her head was tilted back, breasts cupped in the yellow material jutting forward. Her nipples were hard, and Gage ran his tongue over his bottom lip as he imagined taking them in his mouth.

Pumping furiously in and out of her now, he felt his arousal stretching to painful proportions behind the material of his trunks. Her arms had begun to shake; hair that had been pulled up into a messy bun had escaped and now flowed freely down her back. She moaned again, this time long and loud as her legs tightened around him and her nails pressed hard into the skin of his shoulders. Gage moved his fingers faster inside her, feeling her muscles tighten in an attempt to constrict the motion. Her release came strong and hot over his fingers as she moaned his name before leaning forward and dropping her forehead to his chest.

Seconds later and with his fingers still inside her, Gage heard her whisper, "If I'd known this was what a swim lesson consisted of, I may have signed up sooner."

Gage chuckled. He pulled his fingers from her and gripped her hips, letting her legs fall from his waist. When he was sure her feet touched the bottom of the pool, he looked down at her and then hugged her close on impulse.

"I would have offered sooner," he told her.

Much sooner. If he'd known what it would feel like to be with a woman more than once, Gage was certain he would have tried it.

But something told him that it wasn't the number of times that was making the difference. It was Ava.

Chapter 6

Ava felt both at home and out of place at the same time. Morgan's kitchen was homey and welcoming. The soft white cabinets and sage-green paint accented the stainless steel appliances. The countertop full of baby bottles, some empty and some full, a Batman thermos and four covered containers of different sizes kept the country chic design from looking staged.

"My granny loves to cook," Morgan said as she sat across the island from Ava. "The entire time I was pregnant, she talked about all the things she was going to make so that Gray and the kids would have good home-cooked meals while I was recuperating. Whereas my sister Wendy was all set to hit every fast-food and delivery spot in the vicinity to make sure we were fed. The babies are a month old now, and Granny's still sending food over here as if I'm bedridden."

She laughed and Ava smiled. Morgan Taylor was friendly and easy to talk to. She was also observant, Ava thought while finishing the last bite of the fresh-sliced country ham sandwich she'd had for lunch. The invitation from Morgan had come three days after her swim lesson with Gage, and the morning after her second run-in with Millie. The older woman had been with her girlfriends this time, coming out of the library as Morgan walked by. As Otis had already heard about the scene by the time she'd returned to the B and B, Ava figured the lunch invitation was for Morgan to find out firsthand what had happened.

"I never knew my grandparents," Ava replied and used a napkin to wipe her mouth and fingers. "My father's parents did not care for my mother, and by relation, never wanted to see me. And my mother's parents were deceased before I was born."

"Oh, that's sad. I'm sorry," Morgan said. She reached a hand across the table to touch Ava's.

The diamond ring on Morgan's left hand was more like a blinding rock of ice glittering up at her. It should have been too opulent for Morgan's small hand and wholesome personality, but it wasn't. Instead, Ava looked down at the ring and then up to Morgan and saw the love this woman had for her family. In turn, Gray Taylor had shown his love for his wife with this extravagant ring and the loving renovations to this house. It was sweet and on a level of emotion that Ava couldn't really understand.

"Thank you, but it worked out. I kind of liked being an only child, as well, and not having to attend any of the family functions my classmates always complained about," Ava told her.

There'd always been a fear of more people sharing her mother's thoughts and narrow-minded nature. With that in mind, Ava had been totally fine with not having any relatives to deal with.

"Well, we're all about functions here in Temptation. And everyone around town is just like family. Or they like to think they are," Morgan said.

"You're talking about what happened with me and Millie," Ava said when Morgan had pulled her hand away and settled back on the stool. "I'm not sure how all that came about."

Morgan waved a hand. "Millie planned it, that's how. That's what she does. You've been in town for two weeks and everyone's been buzzing about the TV producer who knows the Taylors. It's a wonder she hadn't gotten to you before now."

That made sense. When Millie had approached Ava at her car, it had been with a sugary sweet smile and wintry cool eyes.

"I did get the impression that she'd been waiting to speak to me again," Ava added. "The first words out of her mouth were 'So you're the one who works with Gage Taylor. What else are you two cooking up?' If I wasn't already used to dealing with the press on occasion, I might not have been prepared for the unannounced verbal assault."

Morgan chuckled. "I'm sure that's exactly what it

was, a verbal assault. Millie has a mouth on her, and she doesn't care what anyone else has to say, she's going to speak her piece every time."

"That's fine, but I hope she hears as well as she talks. I made it clear to her once more that Gage and I worked on *Doctor's Orders* together and that I was just here on a writing retreat."

"Oh, I'm sure you did," Morgan said. "That's just not what Millie wants to hear. But it seems like you have the right attitude where Millie's concerned."

"She can think what she wants," Ava told her. "People always do."

"That is certainly true."

Water boiled on the stove, and Morgan slipped off the stool to tend to it. Ava watched as she poured the boiled water into a plastic jug and then put those lidded containers into a shopping bag. Probably to go back to her Granny.

"I don't care what these new formulas call for, I still do it the old-fashioned way—boiling my water first." She smiled. "Never could manage breast-feeding, especially not with twins."

Ava smiled in return and continued to watch curiously until Morgan returned to her seat and picked up her glass.

"Does Gray want more children?"

Morgan choked on the water she'd just sipped.

"Not now," Ava said, reaching to hand Morgan a napkin. "I'm sorry, I should have been clearer. I just mean overall, does he want a big family like his parents had?"

"No," Morgan said, shaking her head. "Gray doesn't

want any of the things his parents had. Neither does Gage or their youngest sister, Gia. Garrek, Gemma and Gen think differently about what happened."

"That's Genevieve, right?"

Morgan nodded. "They used to call her Vivi when they were younger, but after their mother passed, Gray said she wanted to be called Gen. It was too hard to hear the nickname her mother had given her, I suppose."

From all her research, Ava had surmised that the Taylor children suffered traumatically from the early events of their lives. A part of her ached for them.

"When Theodor left, the siblings were emotionally split down the middle. Three of them sided with Olivia, while the other three held back from taking a side at all. Gage and Gia stuck close as the two youngest, but from what Gray has told me, they were adamant that their father never be forgiven for what he did to their family."

"That must have been hard," Ava said, thinking of Gage.

"You know about the Taylors of Temptation, don't you? You would have looked into Gage's past before you hired him. Isn't that how it works?"

Morgan was a schoolteacher, but she asked questions like a trained investigator. Not overtly like a police interrogation, but with an easy flow that garnered the information she wanted. Ava had only to decide whether Morgan's inquisitiveness meant she was a friend or foe in the quest to get the contract signed.

"I did," Ava replied. Again, she was telling a partial truth. She'd only looked into Gage's past a few weeks ago. "But nothing told of the emotion. I mean, there's the story of what happened and that's it. The allegiances, the toll this entire situation took on this family was not easily surmised in any of the stories I read."

"It can't be," Morgan said with a shake of her head. "Their grief is real and raw, and it lives inside them every day. Not just with the death of their parents, but also with reliving the demise of their family. That's what hurt them most. And at the same time, it's what holds them together."

"I understand," Ava said.

"Do you? Because if you do, you'll know that falling in love is not going to be easy for Gage. But when he does, he's going to fall with all his heart. Are you ready for that?"

"What? Why are you asking me that? I'm just here for a—"

"For a writing retreat, I know," Morgan said with a knowing look. "Of all the places in the world, you picked this town. And you picked it after you'd been working with Gage. I've seen how the two of you look at each other. At dinner on my deck that first night, and again at the wine festival when we finally showed up."

"Morgan, I think you're mistaken."

Morgan shook her head. "I don't think I am. But, to be fair, I hope you're getting lots of writing done while you're here."

The sound of crying poured into the room, and both women stared at the baby monitor sitting on the counter near the refrigerator.

"Duty calls," Morgan said cheerily. "I'll be right back."

Ava nodded, and the moment she was alone she let her head fall forward to rest on the cool surface of the island. She groaned with her eyes closed as she replayed the conversation. Morgan wasn't buying her being here for a writer's retreat. Was that good or bad? Was she going to tell Gray? And if she did, how was Gage going to react when he found out she'd been lying to him and his family?

"Well, look who stepped out of her writing lair."

Ava wanted to groan again. She wanted to slink out of this kitchen and take herself back to LA as quickly as possible.

"Hi!" she said instead, in a voice that was way too happy for the way she was actually feeling.

"Haven't seen you out and about in a few days," Gage said while walking farther into the kitchen.

"Ah, no. I mean, I've been out. Just trying to get some writing done. But I do come out and walk around town. I like seeing the sights and the people."

She was babbling, so she snapped her lips closed and stared at him instead. He looked good. Of course he did. Gage always looked good. Jeans and polo shirts had never actually appealed to her before, but on him, they were hot.

"That's great. I've been sort of busy, too."

"Oh, really?"

"Yes. Don't sound so surprised." He chuckled as he took a bottled water out of the refrigerator and opened it.

"Well, you are on vacation, right? And your fast *Playboy* car has been heard zooming on the streets around town. Otis told me that." Ava smiled at the recollection.

Otis had come to her room with a tray of lemonade and Nana Lou's sugar cookies that day. He made a point of visiting her while she was writing, always bringing snacks and tidbits of town gossip. He was a thoughtful but nosy man, and she liked him.

"Fast *Playboy* car, huh? For the record, it's a Jaguar XE, and she is pretty sweet when she gets going," he said before taking a drink.

Ava could watch him for days. Whether he was falling on his butt during a volleyball game, or lounging on a blanket in a park, he was very easy on the eyes. And she liked the way he looked back at her.

"You and your women," she said with a smirk.

"Hey, Gage," Morgan said, returning to the kitchen with an adorable bundle of baby wrapped in a blue Baby Mickey blanket. "Where's Gray? He said you two were meeting with a new doctor at the hospital and then he was coming home to relieve me."

Gage set the bottle on the counter and went to Morgan, gingerly taking the baby from her arms.

"That's why I'm here. To deliver a message. Gray's tied up with an overseas conference call. He'd planned to take it here at the house, but his assistant confused the times, and he had to get on the call in one of the offices at the hospital."

"But I have a meeting with Mrs. Camby about the Fall Festival. She's been the chair of this festival for the last fifty years and never leaves her house for a meeting. I don't really want to take the twins over there."

Gage had been smiling down at baby Ryan, rubbing a finger over the child's small hand. "JoEllen Camby?"

"Yes," Morgan replied. She picked her cell phone up off the counter and started scrolling on it. "Wendy's doing a double shift at the hospital today, and Granny has the food drive at the church. You remember Mrs. Camby?"

"Not really," Gage answered. "She and my mother kept in touch after we left. I remember seeing cards come in the mail from her."

"Oh," Morgan said. "Well, you two are in luck because I need a babysitter."

"A babysitter?" Ava asked.

Morgan nodded. "Yes. Two babies and two of you. I should only be gone an hour. Nana Lou is picking Jack and Lily up after school to take them to Movies and Games Day at the community center. So you won't have to worry about them."

Ava looked over at the baby Gage was holding. He looked pretty comfortable with the little boy in his arms. Ava, on the other hand, felt a wave of panic. "I've never watched a baby before."

She'd never even held one.

"I'll teach you." Gage winked at her.

Morgan looked from him to Ava with a raised brow. "Uh-huh, right. Okay. So it's time for them to be fed. Their next bottles are ready and on the counter over there. I'll finish the new formula when I get back. Ryan always wants to go first. I've already changed him. Emma's going to be up in a few minutes because she doesn't let Ryan get too much of a head start. When she wakes up, just change her diaper. Gage, give Ava my cell number. Call me if there's an emergency, and thank you both so much!"

Morgan was out of the kitchen in a blur of blue sweatpants and hoop earrings. Ava didn't know what to say.

Gage came to stand in front of her. He was so close she could smell the baby scent of Ryan, even though she resisted the urge to look down at what she knew was a bundle of cuteness.

"First things first," he said. "I don't have women. My car is *Jezebel*, and my yacht is *Seraphine*. Those are the only ladies in my life."

"Oh," was all Ava could manage as a reply.

Then her cell phone rang, and Emma's cry blasted through the intercom. Pulling the phone out of her back pants pocket, she frowned when she saw Jenner's name on the screen.

"Okay, well, I guess I'd better get…ah, both of these," she said and then repeated Morgan's previous quick exit.

She needed to get away from the extremely comfortable-looking scene of Gage holding a baby and still looking sexy. And also of Gage telling her that he didn't have a woman…so what was she?

Had she been jealous?

Gage walked to the counter and picked up one of the bottles. He removed the top and placed the nipple between Ryan's small lips. This was his nephew, a new generation of Taylor children. That made Gage smile.

Even while his mind circled back to the way Ava had said "you and your women."

He'd felt the need to clarify the women in his life, and in doing so he realized how lonely it sounded. So he didn't have a significant other. Was that such a big deal? She didn't either—or did she? It occurred to him that between their sexual tête-à-têtes and declaring that there was nothing serious between them, they had never verified that they were each available for such dalliances.

They were adults; that's what mattered. Any agreements they made were mature and thought out. There was nothing to regret.

Then why had he felt like a complete ass when she mentioned his women?

"What do I do now?" he asked, looking down into the innocent eyes of his nephew.

Of course Ryan didn't answer, and after a few seconds Gage wondered why he was even asking. Not his nephew, but himself. There was nothing between him and Ava that he should be wondering about. Hadn't he told himself that in the last few days when he'd been so immersed in the work at the hospital?

"What are you doing staying here so late? Shouldn't you be out with Ava?" Gray had asked last night when they'd both been working late.

"No. I'm not the married one, big brother," Gage had replied.

"Nope, your situation is worse," Gray had stated. "It's the dating phase. You have to work much harder on that part of a relationship."

Gage had shaken his head so hard, his neck had ached. "Not in a relationship either."

Gray's head had tilted back as he'd laughed. "Come on, Gage. You're smarter than that. Why else do you think she followed you here?"

"She didn't follow me and we're not dating," he'd replied.

"If you say so. But you've been seen at the wine festival together and then again at the community center. We can call those outings, but that's just a soft word for dates."

"She's…we…it's not serious." That was all that Gage had managed to come up with.

"Yet," Gray had stated. "And don't tell me you're not the marrying kind because I know better. There's no such thing. A man can commit when he wants to."

"I'm perfectly capable of committing, Gray. I've been committed to my career for the last ten years. That's not where Ava and I are headed," he'd said with finality because he desperately needed to believe it.

Now, Gage wasn't so sure.

When Ryan finished with his bottle and burped like a sixteen-year-old kid, Gage grabbed the second bottle and went upstairs to check on Ava.

Her cell phone was lying in the crib beside a pink Baby Minnie Mouse blanket that resembled the one wrapped around Ryan. She was leaning into the crib grumbling something as she pulled light green pants onto Emma. His niece gave a little cry, and Ava froze momentarily. He watched the rise and fall of her shoulders as she looked down at the baby and finally reached for the blanket. She wrapped her gently and then scooped her up into her arms.

"I don't know what I'm doing, so I'm gonna need you to take it easy on me," Ava whispered to Emma. "Now, we're gonna forget about the mean man on the phone and go downstairs to get your bottle. How do you like that?"

Emma made a gurgling sound and Ava chuckled. "I figured you'd agree with that part. Okay, let's go."

"Who was the mean man on the phone?" he asked before he could consider whether or not he should.

"Oh." She looked startled to see him.

She was holding Emma in one arm as she reached for the cell phone and slowly stuffed it into her back pocket.

"It was nobody," she said with a slight shake of her head. "I mean, nobody important. Just work."

Gage nodded, even while churning over the realization that he didn't like the thought of some guy being mean to her. Add that to his great dislike of other guys holding Ava's hand and Gage knew he was in trouble. He cleared his throat before speaking again.

"Well, I guess I won't have to teach you how to change a diaper after all."

"I figured it out," she told him with a slight chuckle.

Gage held up the bottle he was holding.

"You brought her bottle?" Ava asked.

"I did," he said. "Let's sit here."

The nursery was painted a very pale green with bold white stripes on one side, and pastel-colored balloons on the other. All the furniture in the room was white, including the matching gliders that faced a bay window, which opened to the front of the house.

He waited for Ava to sit before handing her the bottle. Then Gage took the seat next to her.

And there they sat for Gage didn't know how long, rocking the babies and looking out the window.

She didn't say a word and neither did he. Ryan was warm as Gage cuddled him in his arms. Beside him he could hear Ava making cooing sounds at Emma. It struck him then that this was a cozy scene. A scene he'd held in his mind for longer than he cared to admit.

His parents probably sat in this same room looking out the window all those years ago. And now, something clicked inside of Gage. It slipped into a place in his chest as if it had been the missing piece to a puzzle, and he almost sighed because it was finally where it belonged.

Just the way Theodor and Olivia probably had thirty years ago.

Chapter 7

"It's just a leave of absence, Mortimer," Gage said into the phone as he sat in the room he'd been occupying at Harper and Garrek's house. "I'll be back the first of the year."

"I thought this was just a three-week vacation," Mortimer Gogenheim replied. "What about your research? The grant?"

Gage had thought this all through after he'd left Gray's house last night and returned to this room. He'd stayed up half the night thinking of nothing else.

"I'll have weekly Skype calls with the research assistants. In addition, they'll send me weekly reports. I'll review everything, do my own analysis and decide what steps need to be taken next. We're not close to any clinical testing, so me being out of the lab for another two months isn't going to harm the research at all," Gage assured his boss.

"My last day is the end of this week," Mortimer said. "I believe Ed planned to meet with all department staff before then. I told him you would be back because that's what you told me when you left."

Gage kept his gaze on the huge trees swaying with the wind just a few feet away from the window. Leaves drifted in the air before circling down to rest on the grass.

"There have been some new developments." Gage cleared his throat. "Things relating to my father's estate. I have to take care of them before I can return. If it's necessary, I can call and speak with Rodenstein myself."

Mortimer didn't immediately respond.

"If there's something else going on, you can tell me, Gage. Is this about Ed getting the chief position instead of you?"

"I'm not that petty, Mortimer. I'm a professional, always. And I'm committed to my job. I have been for the last ten years. Which is why requesting a leave of absence to deal with my father's estate should not be an issue. But if it is, please let me know and I will deal with it accordingly."

"This just isn't like you," Mortimer said before agreeing to let Dr. Rodenstein and the rest of the staff know that Gage was officially taking a leave of absence.

For the next few hours, Gage thought about Mortimer's words. This *wasn't* like him. Since the day he'd decided to become a doctor, Gage had put nothing else before achieving that goal. And really, he told himself, he wasn't actually pushing his career aside this time. Designing and staffing the obstetrics and infertility research sections of the new Taylor Generational Wing at All Saints Hospital was an extension of his career. It was in his field and correlated perfectly with his work in New York. As such, in the last weeks, Gage had thrown himself wholeheartedly into the project.

He'd also spent more time with Ava Cannon than he had with any other woman, ever.

That thought reminded him of the text message he'd sent to her this morning, inviting her to dinner tonight. It also meant he had a lot to do before the time for said dinner arrived.

After packing the last of his clothes in the leather duffel bag he'd brought with him when he arrived in Temptation, Gage took the bag off the bed and stood in the room, looking around. It was a nice room in the old antebellum home that his father had left to Garrek, and that Harper was now restoring. The stately structure sat on multiple acres of luxurious land, and when finished, would be grand and gorgeous. Harper was really good at her job, even if Gage wasn't a fan of the ornate antique furniture in this particular room.

"Oh, are you leaving?" Harper asked when Gage was headed to the front door.

There was noise, as always here, with work being done on some part of the house every day. So he hadn't heard her approach.

"Hey, Harper. I thought you'd already be out on some other job by now," Gage said as he set his bag on the floor and faced his soon-to-be sister-in-law.

"I'm working here today," she told him. "Have to find some time to put into my own house. Especially if I want to have it finished by the time Garrek comes home."

"He's anxious to return," Gage said. He'd spoken to Garrek a couple days ago when his brother had called to ask why he was in Temptation.

His sisters had also called him because nothing was ever a secret between the Taylor siblings. What one knew, they all knew.

Harper beamed at his words. "But you're leaving? Your vacation is over."

"Actually, I'm not leaving Temptation just yet. I've decided to stay here awhile longer to help Gray at the hospital."

"Yes, with the generational wing. That's fabulous. So why are you packed like you're leaving town?"

"Since I drove my car down, I had to have my yacht shipped here. It's arrived, and I'm just going to stay there for the duration of the trip. As I'm sure you're aware, it gets kind of loud here sometimes, and it's easier for me to work where it's quiet."

Harper chuckled. "That's putting it politely. I know it's loud all the time, and I apologize."

"No need for an apology. It was generous of you to let me stay here, and this was better than intruding on Gray and Morgan with the kids and their schedules. I'll just be down at the dock, but still in town for family dinners and things like that."

"Good, I know that Gray seems really happy you're

here. And Garrek is, too. He only wishes he could be here with all of us."

Gage wished that, too. Quite a few times this week, he'd wondered how it would feel for all of them to be back here in Temptation.

"In due time," he told Harper. "We'll all be together in due time."

The words had reminded him of his mother. Once the siblings had entered high school, they'd often asked Olivia when she was going to do something for herself. They'd all agreed they wanted to see their mother happy, even if they couldn't agree on who or what would get her to that point. Olivia had only smiled and told them, "All in due time."

Now, hours later, Gage was on the luxury super yacht he was currently leasing. The *Seraphine* looked big and a bit ostentatious anchored along Temptation's weathered dock, but Gage didn't care. He loved nice things. They were the one indulgence he afforded himself as a reward for all his hard work. His condo, car and the yacht were like Gage's children, he thought dismally.

It was just about five thirty, and he'd already showered and changed into smoke-gray slacks and a lighter gray button-front shirt. He kept clothes on the yacht, so his decision to stay here longer wouldn't call for a trip to the mall.

"Helloooo down there! I say helloooo!"

Gage smiled at the sound of her voice. Ms. Pearl Brimley was a lovely woman with a wide, friendly smile and deep dimples in each mocha-hued cheek. Gage had stopped at Ms. Pearl's Diner on his way to the yacht and put in an order for dinner to be delivered here for tonight.

"Hellooooo!"

"Coming, Ms. Pearl," Gage answered as he stepped up onto the deck.

Ms. Pearl was standing on the dock, a large square-shaped warming bag in each hand. She wore a blue-and-white-striped skirt that stopped at her ankles and swayed in the breeze.

"Here, let me help you down," he told her as he went to the edge of the deck.

He unhitched the latch that kept the swinging door closed and reached up to take the bags from Ms. Pearl's hands.

"Gail and Meg are right behind me with the rest of the stuff. We'll get you all set up here," she said when Gage turned back to offer her a hand down.

"You said six o'clock, so we'll have to move quickly. But we'll get it all done."

In seconds Ms. Pearl's daughter, Gail, and her niece, Meg, came on board carrying more packages.

"This is so nice," Meg crooned. "I've never seen a boat like this before."

"That's because it's a yacht," Gail replied with a shake of her head.

"Just like the one in the pictures of Jay-Z and Beyoncé on vacation," Meg continued as she unpacked utensils and napkins from the bags she'd carried on deck.

Gage smiled and explained to Meg what type of yacht this was, and that, no, he was not as rich as Jay-Z and Beyoncé. Ms. Pearl beckoned them both back to work, and by five minutes to six, the three ladies were gone and the small bronze pedestal table at the far end of the boat was decorated beautifully.

At three minutes after six, Gage was standing at the door of the deck once more, smiling up at Ava as she stepped slowly onto the yacht.

"You look beautiful," he said, taking her hand to help her on board. "I'm so glad you're here."

And he was, Gage thought as he looked down into her deep brown eyes. He was glad to see her in the short blue dress that might have seemed plain on anyone else but her. She wore a blue-and-beige scarf draped around her neck and black boots to her calf. Her hair was free and flowing so that she had a fresh and innocently enticing look. Yes, he was glad she was here.

"I almost didn't come," she said and then shook her head as if trying to dismiss the words. "I meant to say, thank you. I'm looking forward to a great evening."

He heard the words and saw the small smile she offered, but Gage wasn't buying it. Her eyes and the slight slump in her shoulders said differently.

"Is something wrong, Ava? Did something happen to you today?"

"No," she said and waved her hand over her face like she needed to wipe away whatever was bothering her. "I'm fine. It's nothing. Let's just have dinner."

"Sure. Everything's ready," Gage told her.

He led her to the table and pulled out the matching bronzed iron chair, all the while thinking that she was a horrible liar. Something was definitely wrong with her, and he was determined to find out what.

So he could fix it. Gage knew in that instant that he would do anything to take that look off her face. Anything at all.

She was being ridiculous.

It was unlike her and she hated it.

No, it was just like her after speaking to her mother. That's what she hated more.

Ava took a deep breath, smelled the crisp evening air and looked out to the glistening surface of the water.

"It's nice here," she said quietly. "Who goes on vacation and has their yacht shipped to them?"

The last was said with a wry chuckle as she tried to shake the anger and sadness she'd carried with her for the last hour since her mother's call.

"I wanted to be comfortable since I plan to stay a little longer."

He had just slid onto the chair across from her. For too many torturous moments, he'd stood staring at her, waiting for her to tell him what was going on. Or waiting to figure it out for himself.

Ava turned slightly, hanging her purse on the side of the chair, and then turned back to face him. "How long are you staying now?"

"Through the holidays."

She folded her hands in her lap. "So you'll be here for Morgan's big Christmas dinner. Are the rest of your siblings coming?"

"Yes," he replied. "Morgan, apparently, is very persuasive."

"That should be nice. A family holiday." Ava couldn't help it.

She had decided that she wanted to be in Temptation for Christmas, as well. She wanted to attend the Harvest Brunch and then the Thanksgiving parade in November. And Morgan had told her about her annual class play at the community center. They hadn't chosen which Christmas story they would do this year yet, but Lily and Jack had been so animated last night, when they'd reenacted parts of last year's *A Christmas Carol*, that Ava knew she wanted to see anything those two acted in this year. And all of the Taylors had agreed to come back to Temptation for Christmas. Ava did not want to miss that.

She looked out to the water then and sighed heavily, recalling the earlier conversation with her mother.

"I mean, really, Ava, how long are you going to continue playing at this? May I remind you that you are not getting any younger? When I was your age, I was already married to your father and trying to get pregnant."

"I'm not thinking about marriage and children right now, Mother," she'd said through clenched teeth.

The fact that she'd thought of nothing else but the sweet smell of Emma and Ryan in her arms last night was something she'd keep to herself.

"That's my point exactly. You should be. It's time to stop wasting time with this writing thing and get on with your life."

"This writing thing has resulted in the number one

rated procedural drama last season. It's making a name for me within the industry and opening new doors for my career." At least she hoped what she was doing here in Temptation would do just that.

"Richard is preparing for a third run to keep his Senate seat. He needs your help on the campaign. Now, how soon can you get back to LA? I've already set up some meetings with my committees. They'll support as always, but I need you to get to the young people."

Richard McClain had been the Cannon family lawyer for as long as Ava could remember. Five years ago he had decided to run for Congress and had been elected in a surprise landslide. After Ava's father's death, Richard had been there offering his support to the family, which Ava had appreciated, so she did feel a bit of loyalty to him.

"I'm working and will not be finished with this until at least the first of the year," Ava had said.

"That's just not acceptable, Ava. Not at all. I want you to stop this foolishness right now. I've put too much time and energy into raising you right for you to wander off into some la-la land now."

Ava hadn't been aware that a successful producing career was considered la-la land.

"Look, Mom, I have to go. I have a da…I mean, a meeting tonight. So I'm going to have to call you in the morning."

"Ava, you will not keep putting me off. Now, I told Richard you would be back to help him, and I expect you to honor that agreement."

"I didn't agree to that," she'd replied.

"Do not disrespect me!" Eleanor had yelled.

The sound of her mother taking a deep breath and releasing it very slowly had echoed through the phone, and Ava rolled her eyes. Her mother had perfected the wounded woman act over the years, but this time Ava was prepared.

"I would never disrespect you, Mother. But I really do have to get to this meeting. We can talk more in the morning, I promise. Have a good night," she'd said before clicking off the call.

It wasn't hanging up if she said goodbye, or goodnight. Her father had told her that. It was a long time before Ava suspected it was because he'd hung up on Eleanor plenty of times in his life.

"Ava?"

It was his hand resting on her shoulder more so than the sound of his voice that jolted Ava from her memory and almost out of the chair.

"Are you all right?" Gage asked as he stooped down beside her.

He took her hands then, holding them between his as he stared up at her.

"Whatever it is, you can tell me, Ava. Tell me, so I can help."

She tilted her head, the corner of her mouth moving upward slightly. "You would try, wouldn't you? For as much as you like to give the impression that you're all about your professional life, there's a softer side to you, Gage. A side that wants to make things right for everybody."

"I just don't like the look in your eyes or the tone of your voice right now. Whatever I can do to help, I will."

"You came to work on the set of my show to help," she said. "Even when you wanted nothing more to do with TV networks. And you came back here to help your brother at the hospital. You're always helping."

"Fine. I'm always helping. So let me help you."

She shook her head. "It's nothing," Ava said.

"You're a terrible liar."

Those words were like icicles gliding over her skin. Gage had no idea how good a liar she actually was.

"It's childish and pointless," she said and then sighed because her head was starting to throb. "Just a silly argument with my mother. You know, like everyone has with their parents at some point."

His gaze remained steady. "Not me."

Great, now she really felt like an idiot. Here she was complaining about her mother when both Gage's parents were gone.

"I'm sorry. Let's just forget I even said anything." She tried for a genuine smile. "Guess I'm ruining our date. Is this a date?"

He grinned. "Let's dance."

"What? There's no music."

Gage was already tugging her from the chair. He slipped his arm around her waist and stepped closer, until their bodies were touching. Ava lifted her arms to lock around his neck and joined him when he began to sway. He smelled so good, like very expensive cologne and sexy man. And even though he wasn't holding her too tightly, she felt safe in his arms. Protected. Comforted.

Guilty.

"My mother used to say that dancing cures everything. The movement chases away old ghosts and prevents worries from piling up in your mind."

Ava sighed and let herself focus solely on moving.

"I'm just trying to do my job," she said softly. "All I've ever wanted to do is write. Not be some twenty-first-century debutante in search of a rich husband to continue some society circle nonsense."

His fingers splayed over her lower back, rubbing lightly as he stepped and moved, turning them in a small circle.

"She hates everything about me. Always has," Ava continued. She didn't know why. The words just tumbled free. "Nothing I've ever done has been good enough for her. Probably because I'm not like her. I prefer to drive an economical hybrid car instead of the expensive vehicles she travels in. I live in a reasonably priced condo and not a mansion, which, thanks to my inheritance from my father, I could absolutely afford. I'm not really into flashy things or people with titles and prestige. I just want to write my stories and live a normal life. Is that so much to ask?"

He kissed the top of her head and then waited until she lifted her chin to stare up at him.

"No. It's not," he told her. "You should be able to be whoever and whatever you want to be. That's what my mother used to tell us. It's why she wanted out of the television show. Because she thought it was creating a persona for us that we had no say in. We were stars before we even knew what that meant, or if it was something we wanted in our lives."

"You were doing what they wanted you to do because at the time you didn't have a choice," she said.

She wanted Gage and his siblings to have a choice this time. The same way she had made a choice to write instead of following her mother's plans for her life.

"Your mother did the right thing," she said.

"And your mother thinks she's doing the right thing, too," he replied. "You just have to stand your ground so that she knows her idea of what's right for you is not in your plan."

"I did," she told him. "I have so many times before. She just refuses to listen."

"Then that's her problem, Ava. It's not yours, so don't beat yourself up about it. You have a right to try this your way."

He looked so good staring back at her with his neatly trimmed goatee, thick brows and mesmerizing gaze. She couldn't have written a better scene where a declaration of love would come and happy-ever-after would ensue. Her heart tripped at the thought.

"If this were a date, I'd suggest we skip the meal and head straight to the bedroom," she said nervously.

Yes, she was nervous. Which was ridiculous, because she'd had sex with Gage before.

"Or it might be the part where I whisk you into my arms and carry you to the bed. I'd lay you down and peel your clothes from you slowly, taking the time to touch every part of your naked body, watching your reaction as I did."

She licked her lips and swallowed hard. "Oh, really? And then what would you do? If this were a date, I mean?"

They were still dancing, swaying in the cool evening breeze on the deck of his yacht. That's why she felt dizzy. No other reason.

"After touching every part of your body with my fingers, I would switch places. Using my tongue to taste you." His voice had lowered to a deep timbre.

"I would watch you ride high on the wave of pleasure, then crest and fall with your climax."

Her body tingled all over, her breasts swelling as she pressed closer to him. He was hard. She could feel his erection as surely as she felt the rise and fall of his chest.

"And…then," she whispered, the words trailing off as he'd begun to lower his face to hers.

"Then I would slip inside you, filling you, taking you," he said before brushing his lips over hers.

"Yes," she replied and kissed him back, dragging her tongue over his bottom lip.

Gage chuckled. "Yes what?"

She nipped his lip with her teeth and then sucked it into her mouth, before thrusting her tongue inside to dance along with his.

"Yes, this is a date," she said when they finally broke for air.

He nodded and then bent to pick her up. When she

was in his arms, Gage leaned in, brushing his lips over hers again. "Good. Because I'm ready for the touching and tasting to begin."

Chapter 8

He did just what he said he would, and Ava was profoundly grateful.

She was also more aroused than she'd ever been before.

Gage had carried her across the deck and down a spiral set of stairs. The bed was huge on this luxurious vessel. She hadn't expected anything less. From the moment she'd received his message to meet him at the docks and then stepped out of her car at the parking lot across the street, she'd known the *Seraphine* was going to be like nothing she'd ever experienced. She'd never been on a yacht before, the whole not-knowing-how-to-swim thing holding her back from cruises of any sort. Tonight, she was glad she'd pushed that anxiety aside.

He gently laid her on the king-size bed and first removed her boots. Propped up on her elbows now, Ava looked around briefly. The walls were dark, a mixture of blue and gray in a textured paper that reminded her of a deep blue sea. A crystal-covered lamp was on each nightstand, and beige carpet covered the floor. Gage's hands moved slowly up her bare calves and farther, until his fingers grazed the sensitive skin between her thighs.

Her attention solely on him now, she watched with anticipation as he pushed at the material of her tunic dress. He looked up at her and winked just before hooking his fingers in the band of her panties and tugging. Ava lifted her hips, allowing him to remove the white silk underwear she'd worn without question. Her scarf went next, and then he was pulling the dress up and over her head.

She was sitting up now, Gage kneeling with one knee between her spread legs, the other on the opposite side of her thigh. He leaned in, reached around her back and unsnapped her matching bra. Cool air hit her nipples, and they hardened seconds before his fingers brushed over them. She sucked in a breath and thought he may have done the same, before he pulled his hands away.

Backing off the bed now, Gage began to undress. She'd seen him naked before so that wasn't the reason for the immediate pounding of her heart. They'd had sex before, so the anticipation of that act was not making her anxious. It was the slowness with which he moved that had her skin tingling. Her eyes were riveted to his every move.

His long fingers moved precisely over each button on his shirt and continued to work steadily to undo his belt and then the snap and zipper of his pants. The shirt and the undershirt he'd worn beneath were removed first, so that when he bent down to tend to his shoes, Ava saw the muscles of his shoulders leading down to his back. He stood when his shoes were off and pushed his pants and boxer briefs down his muscled legs. Ava didn't move, even though a wicked storm of desire was brewing inside her.

"I want to touch you," Gage said as he kneeled on the bed once more. "Lie back and let me touch you, Ava."

She did as he said, hadn't even thought of not complying. His voice was low, so much so that she almost strained over the pounding of her heart to hear him.

He lifted each of her feet, kissing the arch and then the tips of her toes. He rubbed her calves once again, taking each leg in his hands and kissing behind her knee. Her fingers clenched the duvet beneath her as prickles of pleasure soared from each spot he touched throughout her body. When he came to her thighs, they'd begun to shake. She couldn't help the movement, nor could she contain the moan when his lips touched her inner thigh.

"So soft," he whispered.

Ava closed her eyes as her entire body began to tremble.

He kissed up the inside of one thigh, stopping just shy of her juncture before pulling away. She wanted to scream, but instead bit her bottom lip.

"Sexy Ava," he said as he went to the other thigh. "You've been tempting me since day one with your voice, your scent, your body."

She was going to explode. She wasn't going to be able to stop it. He was licking little circles over the skin of her inner thigh, moving upward once more until she wanted to lift her hips off the bed and offer herself to him.

"Gage," she whimpered, when he was just inches away from the plump folds of her center. "Please."

He did not oblige. Damn him.

Instead he blew his warm breath over her bare mound, causing her to shiver and groan.

"You're going to be sweet and warm," he grumbled. "I know it before I even taste you. My sweet and sexy Ava."

Oh no, this was taking too long. Ava released the duvet from her death grip and clapped her hands to the back of Gage's head.

He chuckled as he held back from her. "I'm hungry for you, too," he told her. "But we've got all night."

Ava didn't think she was going to last that long.

And she didn't.

The second Gage touched her tender folds, she almost bolted up off the bed. He placed one hand on her hip and used the other to spread her open before licking her up and down. Ava moaned deep and long, her thighs shaking around his head. Gage continued, licking, sucking and praising her sweetness until seconds later her release tore through her body like an earthquake, and she screamed his name.

He only gave her a minute to recuperate before he was moving upward, kissing her abdomen, licking up her torso and then covering one nipple with his mouth, holding the other breast in his hand. Ava arched her back and felt herself climbing steadily toward another climax.

The moment he pulled away to get a condom, she seriously considered screaming for him to come back immediately. That should have been the second clue that she was sinking fast where Gage Taylor was concerned. She never thought about dismissing safe sex.

Sheathed and coming over her like a gorgeous African god, Gage lifted Ava's legs, propped her ankles on his shoulders and speared into her with one swift motion. His name tumbled from her lips again and again as he moved expertly in and out of her. She felt like she was drowning. The pleasure was so deep, going far beyond anything in her wildest imagination, touching a part of her she'd thought did not exist.

"Look at me, Ava," he said.

She thought she'd opened her eyes, but he was asking her again, "Ava, sweetness, please look at me."

Her lids fluttered open. He released her legs, but stayed buried deep inside her, his elbows coming to rest on either side of her head as his thumbs caressed her cheeks.

"You are beautiful and you are enough," he whispered as he began to move inside her once more. "You are more than enough for me."

She wrapped her legs around his waist, her arms around his back, and moved with him.

"Gage," she whispered. "More. More than I ever expected."

"Yes," he replied. "So much more."

He was moving too slowly, going too deep, hitting her every spot just right and then some. He was too much. This was too much. But when they both trembled and fell together, Ava realized with startling clarity that it wasn't enough. Nothing she'd had with Gage so far was enough.

And wanting more was going to crush her.

"I didn't think I was going to like it here in Temptation," Gage told her as they lay in his bed once more.

After making love, they'd showered and had the dinner Ms. Pearl prepared for them while sitting in the center of the bed. It had felt like those nights when the boys and girls in his house would meet up in the kitchen for a late-night snack. Olivia did not like them eating upstairs in their room, so the siblings had to sneak and decided it was safer if they went into one room. Those were some of the best nights of Gage's life.

Now he could add tonight to that list.

"Then why'd you come back?" Ava asked.

They'd enjoyed the delicious, if a bit cold, food and cleaned up, only to lie back in the bed as if they did not have this spacious yacht to lounge upon.

"Responsibilities that I'd put off for way too long. And to see Gray and meet his new family," he said.

"Your brother has a beautiful family," she replied.

They were both lying on their sides, facing each other. Her arm was tucked under her head and her knees pulled up so that she looked almost like a child. Except Gage knew that beneath his New York Yankees T-shirt she now wore, Ava was all woman.

"I didn't think he would get that chance," Gage admitted. "Truth be told, I wasn't sure any of us would want to start a family after what we'd been through."

"Was it really that bad?" Ava asked. "I know your parents split up, but listening to you and Gray talk about your mother, it sounds like she loved each of you with all her heart. And that she gave you a good life."

"She was a great mother. A wonderful woman who deserved more than to end up raising six children on her own."

"Your father didn't help?"

"He sent money and gifts, if that's what you mean by help." Gage grit his teeth and then thought of his conversation with Gray at the hospital. He took a deep breath and released it. "I guess he did what he could. A person can only be who they are, not who or what someone else wants them to be."

She nodded at his words, and Gage hoped that she was retaining them for her own use, as well.

"My mother was the nurturer. She was meant to be a mother. Gemma is that way, too. I hope she finds love and builds a family of her own one day. Gen is tough, so for any man to crack her shell he might need to be a magician." He chuckled at the thought of his older sister.

"Gia has a soft heart. She trusts and sees the best in everyone. Too soon and usually to her detriment, but I think she'll be a great mother one day, too."

"What about you?"

"What about me?"

"Will you be a good father one day?"

Gage let the uneasy feeling that immediately filled his chest settle before replying.

"My father left his children everything he had. His company, real estate and money. I wasn't shocked by how much his estate had been worth or how quickly Gray managed to divide everything up equally amongst us. Gray has always been a good leader. The other money that Gray found did surprise me a bit, and then the pictures. I'm still trying to figure out why he left them for me."

When he caught her looking a little confused, Gage realized what he'd just told her. He couldn't take it back, and he didn't really want to. He hadn't planned on sharing his thoughts and feelings about his father with anyone, but he had. With Ava.

She reached her free hand across the bed to take his. "What were the pictures of?"

"Us," he replied after lacing his fingers through hers. "A four-month sonogram photo of each of us, and one of us after we were born with my parents."

"Maybe he wanted to show you that he'd always loved you. Regardless of what happened, he'd never stopped loving his children or his wife."

"He cheated on her," Gage snapped. "He had an affair with a production assistant and then decided he'd rather be with her than with his family."

His words were cold and stung as he spoke them. He hadn't realized how much animosity he still held inside because of them.

"My father didn't leave us for another woman. He drank," Ava said. "So much that sometimes I don't even think he saw me. He was a partner at a prestigious law firm in LA. He represented so many stars, and sometimes a studio would call on him for contractual work. He had money, houses, cars, everything, and he drank so much that one day he drove his car right off a cliff and into the ocean."

"Dammit, Ava. I'm sorry," Gage said, immediately feeling like scum as he complained about his father.

She smiled. "Don't be. He lived the life he wanted to live, and he drank because of some problem he couldn't figure out how to solve. I wish he had been able to overcome his issues, but I don't hate him for how it ended. And you shouldn't hate your father for things that, in the end, he could not change."

She was right. Gage knew that. And so did Gray. It was time to move past all that hurt he'd clung to, which was why he'd told Gray he didn't think they should continue to pay those investigators to try to figure out where the Grand Cayman money had come from. The money was divided between the children just like everything else Theodor Taylor owned, and that was that.

"Thank you for saying that," he told her. "And for joining me tonight. I know you came here to write. That's why I try not to bother you every second of every day."

But he'd wanted to. He could admit that to himself. During the hours he spent at the hospital, or when he was walking through town or having dinner at some restaurant, he thought about her.

"Oh, it wouldn't be a bother," she said. "I write better in the early-morning hours anyway. By midday I'm already beginning to fade, unless it's crunch time."

"So you're writing new scripts for the next season of the show?"

"Actually, no, I'm writing something new and totally different."

He brought her hand up to his lips and kissed her fingers. "Well, it'll be great whatever it is."

"Yes," she said after a few minutes. "I think it will be great. But right now—"

She paused and leaned over until she could reach the nightstand drawer. She'd seen him retrieve a condom from there earlier, and she pulled a packet from the box now. When she returned to him, it was to push him over onto his back.

"Now it's my turn to touch and taste," she told him as she grabbed his shirt and lifted it up and over his head.

When Gage lay back on the pillow, she straddled him. And when her warm tongue touched his pectoral muscle, he groaned.

She could take her turn…as many times as she wanted.

"Is that how you Hollywood people do the walk of shame?" Millie said the moment Ava stepped off the dock and onto the cement walkway.

The sun was barely up, shimmering over the water in hazy orange-and-red rays when she'd crept off the yacht. Seagulls flew low, bellowing a choking call to whoever else was up this early.

"Good morning, Ms. Millie," she said in as cheerful a voice as she could muster.

The woman had stepped right up to her so that Ava struggled to keep from telling her that she was invading her personal space. Millie's hair was perfectly styled as it had been on each occasion that Ava had seen her. Her makeup was likewise flawless, Millie's red-painted lips drawn in a thin line.

"I was coming to tell Gage Taylor he needs to take this monstrosity back to wherever it was before now. It's bringing unwanted attention down here to the docks where simple folk are trying to make a living."

Ava looked around, even though she was certain there was no one out here right now but her and Millie. To the woman's credit, there were a couple of smaller boats already out to sail not too far from the dock with what Ava guessed were fishermen on board.

"I don't think the yacht is a disturbance," Ava said, taking a chance at responding. "It seems the people who need to go to work are doing just that."

Except for busybody Millie, that was.

"Don't get sassy with me. You're not in California with your snooty friends," Millie snapped.

Ava was certain she didn't have snooty friends. In fact, she could count on one hand how many actual friends she had.

"Well, it was nice seeing you, Ms. Millie, but I have to get going."

"Where to at this time of morning? Because I know you didn't spend the evening on that boat with Gage Taylor writing. I want to know why you're really here,

Ms. Cannon. If it has something to do with this town, I have a right to know."

"My work is my business," Ava said, squaring her shoulders. She had been trying to be polite, but she wasn't going to be bullied by this woman a second time.

"Not if it's taking place in my town. I don't believe for one minute you're just on a writing retreat. Seems too fishy that you and Gage show up at the same time. And you're in the TV business, too. Oh, no, too suspicious." Millie was shaking her head.

Ava smiled. "Ma'am, you can make what you want out of it, but I've told you all that I plan to. Now, you can have a nice day."

Ava skirted around the primly dressed woman and did everything short of breaking out into a run to get to her car. Once behind the wheel and pulling out of the parking lot, Ava thought the first call she was going to make when she returned to the B and B was to Jenner.

The Taylor Reunion reality show was not going to come to fruition, at least not the way he wanted it to.

Chapter 9

Were they really ready for this?

As the limo rode through the streets, taking them to this year's location for the Critics' Choice Awards, Ava thought over the last six weeks of her life. She was in a different place now, somewhere she'd never thought she would be.

"Nervous?" Gage asked.

He was sitting beside her, holding her hand. Dressed in a black Tom Ford suit, his shirt and pocket square crisp white, and sporting shined Ferragamo oxford cap-toe shoes, he looked stylish and delicious even without the help of a stylist. But when they'd arrived at her

LA condo two days ago, Saraya had already called on Ava's friend Landry Norris to get her and Gage ready for the awards show. Now married to the Crown Prince Kristian DeSaunters of Grand Serenity Island, Landry's family still lived in California, and she frequently came home for visits.

"A little," Ava admitted to Gage.

She tightened her fingers around his, seeking and receiving the comfort she'd become slightly addicted to in the past weeks. He was like the rock she hadn't realized she needed in her life. After all these years of depending on herself, relying on her own instincts and discipline to get where she was in life, Ava had never imagined being able to lean on anyone else. Which made what she planned to do in the coming days so much harder.

"Don't be," he told her. "You look stunning and smell amazing. And regardless of what happens tonight, you'll still be the youngest African American writer and producer with a number one rated show on network television right now. Nothing else matters."

Ava inhaled deeply and felt the breath releasing slowly, calmly as she looked into his deep brown eyes. He'd commented on the scent of her perfume the second he'd entered the bedroom after he'd finished dressing. Landry had still been putting finishing touches on Ava—diamond stud earrings and matching cuff bracelet. The Tony Chaaya mermaid-cut black gown Ava wore was gorgeous and made her feel sexy and confident. The messy bun with loose curls around her face was elegant, her makeup flawless, and still her stomach would not settle.

"Thank you," she whispered. "For saying that and agreeing to come here with me. I know you've been really busy with your work at the hospital, and this was sort of last-minute."

He shrugged and smiled. "My schedule's a little flexible at the moment. Besides, this is an important moment for you. I'm honored that you asked me to share it with you."

She had asked him as they'd sat on the steps at Harper's father's farm after a seafood feast. Her agent, Marcelle, had called her that morning to tell her that she'd been nominated. Since she'd been in Temptation, Ava had been basically off the grid, so the news of the nominations hadn't immediately gotten to her.

Now, the night was here and she was nervous about possibly winning in the Best Drama Series category. Corbin Yancy and Miranda Martinez were also nominated in the Best Actor and Best Actress in a Drama Series categories. That gave *Doctor's Orders* a total of three nominations for their first season. It was an amazing accomplishment, one that Ava did not take lightly.

"I especially want to thank you because I know you do not like being in the spotlight," she told him as the car had begun to slow down. "I want you to know that I do respect your feelings about things that happened in your past. I was just thinking that having the experience as an adult may be totally different. But I would have understood if you'd turned me down."

He leaned in and kissed her lips quickly. Just a peck because Landry had warned him about messing up her makeup when they were at the hotel and she'd mentioned how Gage was staring hungrily at Ava.

"I'm here because I want to be here with you. That's it. We're not bringing anything else into this. Got it?"

Ava smiled because if she'd had any doubts or reservations before, she knew now with absolute certainty that she was in danger of falling in love with Gage Taylor. And that was not a good thing; at least it wouldn't be if she continued to put off telling him the truth.

"Got it," she replied just as the car stopped.

They would be walking the red carpet, posing for pictures and talking to reporters. She was ready for this. It was her dream, right? Yes, it was, and she had the best guy here with her, to share her perfect moment. She could do this. She was ready to do this.

And apparently, so was Gage.

He was magnificent, holding her hand as they first stepped onto the red carpet, smiling and posing when cameras were aimed at them. Joking and being cordial with reporters who tossed out questions like, "How long have you two been dating?" and, "Are there wedding bells in the future?" Ava had no idea how they'd even known who Gage was, but when the first reporter had approached them asking, "Mr. Taylor, how does it feel to return to the spotlight after your family's retreat thirty years ago?" Ava had thought Gage would turn back and go to the limo. But he hadn't. He'd answered every question with brutal honesty, cutting the reporters short when their questions became too pushy with a stern, but polite, reply. He was perfect.

And later that evening when they opened the envelope and called Ava's name, her perfect guy had stood and hugged her, whispering, "I am so proud of you," in her ear.

Following the show, they headed to one of the two after-parties Ava was scheduled to attend. Saraya had handled everything from securing their tickets, arranging transportation and even sending Ava and Gage the entire night's itinerary in a detailed text. The first party was at the Viceroy, where Ava and Gage mingled with guests and posed for yet more pictures. Her cheeks had already grown sore from smiling, but adrenaline continued to rush through her each time she was approached by someone else.

Until those someones were Jenner and Carroll, both beaming as they strode toward her. Gage had stepped away to find them something to drink. There was no shortage of champagne and other mixed drinks being floated around by resort staff, but they both wanted water, which was obviously too simple a drink to be offered to guests at this party. She immediately clutched her purse tightly in her hands and straightened her back. There was no doubt Jenner would want to talk to her about their last phone conversation. He hadn't been thrilled with Ava's progress, and she hadn't cared. That bravado seemed a bit easier over the phone; still she was determined not to falter.

"Congratulations, Ava! We did it!" Carroll said before pulling her into a tight hug.

"Yes, we did!" she replied and genuinely returned

his hug because Carroll had taken a chance on her, and she respected and appreciated him for that.

Jenner's hug and congratulations were just a little less exuberant.

"With this feather in our cap, our new project is guaranteed to be a hit," Jenner immediately said.

Carroll was nodding so intently that his jowls shook with the motion. "And you brought him with you. That was a great PR idea! Wish we had come up with it."

Jenner clapped his hands together and smiled gleefully. "It's perfect! The press is loving it. Sending your itinerary for the night and the name of your date to a few key members of the press was a brilliant idea. The buzz is already starting about the Taylors. So we'll be all set to announce the show just before Christmas."

Ava shook her head. "You sent my itinerary to reporters?" she asked. "Are you crazy?"

"No," Jenner said, sobering just a bit. "On the contrary, I count myself as being quite smart. I knew you'd be great for this project."

"I told you it wasn't going to go down the way you planned," Ava said through clenched teeth. They were in a crowded room full of people either trying to get the next big Hollywood scoop, or trying to get a part in the next winning movie or show. None of whom she wanted to overhear this conversation.

"My proposal is going to outline the show, leaving lots of leeway for the siblings to determine the content. My pitch to them is contingent upon their having control over how their lives are presented to the world," she told Jenner. "We discussed this already."

"And I told you we would see about that. As for now, we're starting the beginning publicity rounds. You and Gage embracing when you won that award only adds another layer to the project. We'll get to cover the love interest of one of the siblings, with our very own producer. It'll be like déjà vu," Jenner said, his eyes gleaming with his excitement.

Ava couldn't believe it—he was actually becoming happy about exploiting Theodor Taylor's infidelity, thirty years later, on television.

"That's not the outline I'm going to write," she said adamantly.

Jenner took a step closer to her then, taking her arm and pulling her to him. "You are going to do what I tell you to do. I got stiffed once by Theodor Taylor dying after he'd already signed on for this show, and dammit, I won't get shafted again. Now, you have that proposal to me next week or your career will spiral to an end as quickly as you've soared to the top."

"Is there a problem here?" Gage asked as he joined them.

He was holding two water bottles, but he stuck them in his jacket pockets as he placed a hand on Jenner's shoulder, pushing him away from Ava. He reached behind with his other hand and found Ava's, twining his fingers tightly with hers.

She cleared her throat and made the introductions, to which Gage remained unfazed.

"It's a pleasure to meet you, Dr. Taylor," Jenner said, his boisterous smile in place once again.

Jenner extended his hand to Gage, but Gage made no move to return the shake.

"Yes, it is," Carroll chimed in. "We hope you're enjoying your stay here in Santa Monica. If there's anything we can get you, please do not hesitate to let us know."

"I don't need anything," Gage told them and then looked to Ava. "Are you ready to go?"

"Yes," she replied immediately, not bothering to look at Jenner or Carroll again before walking away.

Gage thought he'd been doing well. But five hours into this glamorous evening full of celebrities, producers, agents and groupies, he'd started to reach his limits. The final push could have been when he'd been in search of their drinks and he'd bumped into a familiar face.

"Dr. Gage Taylor, what a surprise it is to see you out here," Miranda Martinez had said as she'd stepped right up to him.

Her long red-painted nails were a bright contrast to his dark suit jacket as she rubbed her hand down the lapel. Lips painted the same vibrant glossy hue and hair black as night falling in fluffy curls past her shoulders weren't as alluring as they should have been for some reason. She wore a purple gown that left more of her skin exposed than was necessary, and her perfume stung Gage's nostrils.

"Hello, Miranda," he'd said reluctantly. "Congratulations on your nomination."

She pouted, an effort that came across as foolish and almost cartoonish, with her full red lips.

"What do the critics know anyway?" she said. "I mean, they did say we were the best drama series, but that's only because of me."

Right. Gage stepped away from her. "Well, if you'll excuse me—"

She'd cut him off by lifting her hand to cup the back of his neck. "Not so fast. We hardly ever had a chance to really talk while on set. And now you're here. How about we ditch this party and go somewhere a little quieter?"

"No," had been Gage's immediate response. And since she didn't take the response to mean he didn't want her touching him, Gage clasped her wrist and eased her hand away. "I'm going to get Ava something to drink."

"Oh, she looks like she's well taken care of at the moment," Miranda had said before nodding her head in the direction across the room.

That's when Gage had seen the two men boxing Ava in. He'd been instantly irritated. He'd abandoned plans of searching for the water and moved in that direction. One of the staffers stopped him before he could get there, thrusting two water bottles and another beaming smile his way. With a curt "thank you," Gage had taken the water and then went directly to Ava. It was as he'd come closer that he'd seen the man's hand on Ava's arm. Rage as he'd never experienced boiled inside of him, and he'd gone into action.

Now he was holding her hand tightly, moving them

through the crowd as quickly as possible. He wanted to get out of here, away from all these unscrupulous and mean-spirited people. So being stopped again irritated the hell out of him; still, for Ava's sake, he managed another smile.

"Ava Cannon," the man, wearing a navy blue jacket and wide smile standing in front of them, stated.

He was quickly joined by another man of the same stature, but dressed in a dove-gray suit.

"Yes," Ava said, bringing back the smile she'd also kept close this evening. "Hello."

"Hello," the man continued and extended his hand to her. "My name is Parker Donovan, from Donovan Network Television. Let me congratulate you on the big win for *Doctor's Orders* tonight."

"Oh, well, thank you, Mr. Donovan," she replied and eased her hand out of Gage's to shake Parker Donovan's.

"This is my brother, Savian," Parker said, signaling the man beside him.

"Congratulations," Savian said. "My wife watches your show faithfully."

"Oh really? Well, tell her I said thank you."

"I will. She's a lawyer and says it's easier to sit back and watch a show about another profession and their drama than her own," Savian continued with a chuckle.

"Well, my wife might be reading for a spot on your show soon, she's such a fan," Parker added.

"Your wife…wait a minute, Adriana Bennett-Donovan? Is she your wife?" Ava asked. "I've seen her work. She's very talented."

"She is on both counts," Parker replied with a smile

that could only come from a man who really loved his woman.

Gage relaxed at that thought and extended his hand to them. "Hello, I'm Dr. Gage Taylor."

Parker and Savian shook his hand and spoke with a genuine sincerity that Gage hadn't seen much of tonight.

"Were you heading out?" Savian asked.

Ava looked to Gage. He didn't speak, but let her make the decision on her own. This was her night, after all.

"Ah, yes, we are. But I'm so glad we met up with you before doing so," she said warmly.

"I am, too," Parker told her.

"We won't hold you up," Savian said. "But we would be interested in meeting with you."

"Definitely," Parker added. "We're always interested in adding new and innovative shows to our schedule, and you definitely have your finger on the pulse of what viewers want."

Gage saw the surprise on Ava's face and once again took her hand in his, pride swelling in his chest.

"I…I would love the chance to talk further with you," she said. "Ah, I'm heading back to Virginia tomorrow morning, but if you get in contact with my agent, we can definitely set up a mutually convenient time to chat."

Parker nodded. "We'll do that very soon," he said. "Now, you two have a good night."

"Thanks," Gage said with a nod to both men.

"Take care, Ava," Savian said. "We'll speak soon."

"Thank you both. Good night."

They were in the limo when Gage finally pulled

those bottles of water out of his pockets and set them on the bar.

"Well," he said when he sat back against the seat. "You've had a pretty cool night."

"Yeah," she said, still smiling. "I have. And you know what?"

"What?" he asked.

She lifted her hands to cup his face. "It's all because of you."

He tried to shake his head. "No. This has been all about you. I didn't do a thing."

"You were here when I needed you. I'll never forget that, Gage," she said, her voice soft.

He brushed a hand over her hair and leaned in closer. "There's no place I'd rather have been, Ava."

When his lips touched hers, Gage realized how much he meant those words. He wanted to be with Ava. In the morning, on his yacht, in Gray's backyard, on the set in New York and the red carpet in California.

He wanted to be with her. It was that simple and that terrifying at the same time.

Chapter 10

Temptation, Virginia

Four days later, Ava had just finished her final draft of the outline for *The Taylors of Temptation: A Whole New World.* She'd renamed the show and changed it from a full season to a two-hour feature with a focus on each sibling and their reflection on how the original show shaped their current lives.

She'd read it over twice, making sure that she hit each emotional beat possible. In her mind, and after being in Temptation for almost two months now, this was the key to this family. While she hadn't spoken to Gen, Gemma and Gia personally, she'd learned a lot from talking with Morgan and Harper about the sisters. Gray and Gage spent a lot of time at the hospital, but on the nights she was with Gage on the yacht, his memories of his sisters and all the torturous things the brothers did to them during their years in Pensacola were unforgettable. They were the years that the Taylor sextuplets formed their bond. The bond that remained steadfast and unbreakable now, all these years later. That's what she wanted the world to see and to remember this town and these people by.

And she hoped with everything in her that the Taylor sextuplets would go along with her plan. It was the twenty-ninth of October. The Fall Festival was tomorrow. She and Gage were slated to judge the pumpkin-carving contest, and Craig—who insisted that Ava had broken his heart—had selected a perfectly gruesome movie for everyone to watch on the night before Halloween. It was going to be a great time. So she would wait until the family dinner scheduled for the day after the festival at Morgan and Gray's to propose her idea to them. Their agreement was important to her, regardless of what Jenner said. If he wanted the Taylors on television as badly as he said he did, then he would accept any changes the sextuplets wanted to make. And if not...

A brisk knock on her door had Ava almost jumping off the bed where she'd been sitting cross-legged staring at her laptop. She wasn't expecting anyone, and as such, was dressed in old gray leggings and a peach tank top that had certainly seen better days. Before she could get to the door, there was another knock and then a familiar voice.

"Ava Marie Cannon, if you do not open this door

right now, I'll have this man break it down. Although I'm not sure he could as he looks a bit frail."

Ava groaned as she reached for the knob and pulled the door open.

"What are you doing here, Mother?"

"Yes, hello to you, too," Eleanor said.

She'd been holding a handkerchief that she now placed in the palm of her hand. She then used that palm to push the door open farther and enter the room.

Ava sighed and tried counting to ten. Otis stood in the hallway, his baseball cap balled up in one hand, while the other hand scratched the tight graying curls on his head.

"You can go now," Eleanor said to him from behind Ava. "Close the door, Ava."

Ava felt awful. "I'm sorry," she said to Otis.

The man simply shook his head, his leathery almond-toned skin lifting on one cheek as he resisted a smile. "No problem. Was nice meeting you, Mizzus Eleanor Cannon," Otis said as he looked past Ava to her mother.

Ava looked back to find her mother had gone deeper into the room and was now running her handkerchief-covered finger over the top of the dark oak armoire.

"You let me know if you need anything, Miss Ava. I'll be right downstairs," Otis said with a nod to her.

"Thanks, Otis. We should be fine. Have a good night," she told him and waited while he waved and attempted to look farther inside the room once more before closing the door.

Flattening her back against the door, Ava glared at where her mother now stood near the bed.

"Does this place really not have any good hotels? I mean, this is ridiculous, Ava," Eleanor said. But before Ava could answer, she continued. "Well, I guess it is what it is. And that means it's a good thing I'm here. Let's get you packed. I have a driver waiting downstairs to take us to the nearest city with suitable accommodations. Then we can fly out of here as soon as possible."

"I'm not leaving," Ava said almost to herself.

"Where are your suitcases? Come, Ava, don't procrastinate." Eleanor continued to move throughout the room, stopping at the floral-printed couch in the sitting area of the room and scrunching her twenty-five-thousand-dollar nose at it.

"I don't need a suitcase, Mother," Ava said, pushing herself away from the door and walking toward Eleanor. "Because I'm not ready to leave Temptation."

"Well, I certainly am," Eleanor told her as she set her large Givenchy Atigona tote on the coffee table.

For a moment Ava could only stare at the woman who had not only raised her, but had also given birth to her. How could they have been any more different? Was it truly possible that people who shared the same DNA could be any less alike? The answer to that was obvious as she watched Eleanor Germaine Stanley Cannon smooth down the skirt of her winter-white Chanel suit and sit ever so gingerly on the edge of the couch. She was a very fair-skinned woman with auburn-colored hair that dared not ever show a speck of gray, or she would personally choke her hair stylist. Diamonds glittered from the ring fingers on both hands, at her ears and in the choker at her neck. Her pumps were Louboutin, her nails long and perfectly manicured, makeup light but efficient. She was beautiful and cold and the only family Ava had.

"When my work is finished I'll return to LA, then probably back to New York for site-scouting on the show."

"Nonsense, you pay people for that, and I told you Richard is expecting you."

Counting hadn't worked, and deep breaths weren't helping. Words were failing miserably. So that was three for three. Maybe food and a public place would be better.

"I'm hungry," Ava said quickly. "How about we go get dinner and discuss something else. Like, I don't know, maybe how I just received a prestigious award for my show almost a week ago."

She didn't wait for Eleanor's answer, but walked back toward the bed and slipped her feet into the flats she had there. She grabbed a jacket and her purse from the chair on her way to the door, and then turned back to see her mother still sitting with her hands folded primly in her lap.

"Are you coming, or do you want to stay here and have dinner with Mr. Otis?"

"I don't see why we couldn't have the driver bring us," Eleanor complained when she climbed out of the passenger side of the hybrid vehicle. "This…car, or whatever, is horrible. And where are we? Does this place even serve Troubadour Pinot Noir? I need a drink and a medium rare steak."

And Ava needed a tranquilizer and a six-pack. Or maybe a one-way ticket to Budapest, a place she was almost positive her mother wouldn't follow her to.

"It's a nice Italian restaurant, Mother. They have wine and pasta. You like pasta," she said as they walked up to the doors of the Temptation Trattoria.

"Well, hello, Ava. Nice seeing you this evening. I heard about your award. You go, girl!" Niecy Monroe, a tall, slim nineteen-year-old saving money to move to Hollywood to chase her own dreams, worked as a hostess at the restaurant. She and Ava had become fast friends since Niecy admired everything about Ava's life—except Eleanor, Ava was certain.

"Thanks, Niecy. Can we get a booth in the back, please?"

"Sure, sure," Niecy replied and then leaned over the podium and iPad they used to keep their seating chart to whisper, "Is she an exec from Hollywood?"

Ava almost laughed. "No. This is my mother, Eleanor Cannon."

"Oh my, well, hello Mrs. Cannon," Niecy said as she grabbed two menus and led the way to their booth.

"I'll bet you're brimming with pride for Ava. She's so talented and nice. I heard stories about those Hollywood producers being stuck up or mean. Ava's nice and friendly. She's fit right in here in Temptation. Almost like she was born here," Niecy continued as they walked through to the back of the restaurant.

"Well, she was not born here, thank the heavens," Eleanor snapped.

"Oh, well," Niecy said when they were both seated and she attempted to hand Eleanor the laminated menu.

When Eleanor only looked at the girl with a weary expression, Ava accepted the menus, and gave Niecy an apologetic smile.

"Right, so Raquel's your waitress, and she'll be over soon to take your drink order."

"Please tell her that I'd like a glass of Troubadour Pinot Noir. As a matter of fact, just bring us the bottle. We can take it back to that shack where my daughter is staying," Eleanor said without bothering to look at Niecy, who was now frowning.

"Thanks, Niecy," Ava said and waited until the girl was gone before chastising her mother.

"You really don't have to treat them like this. They're nice people here."

Eleanor sighed and reluctantly sat back against the seat. "I'm sure they are, Ava. But this is not what I'm used to. It's not what you were raised to accept. Why you refuse to take advantage of all the things available to you, I have no idea."

"I like doing things my way, Mother. It has nothing to do with you."

"That's what I'm sensing," her mother replied. "That you don't want to have anything to do with me."

"That's not what I meant," Ava said. "I'm just tired of trying to make you see me for who I am. I am not, nor will I ever be, the daughter you planned for. I'm me, and I love and respect you as my mother, but if you don't stop criticizing me and ignoring my accomplishments, our relationship is going to take a bad turn."

There. She'd said it. She'd kept her cool, and she'd maintained a respectful tone, all while telling her mother in no uncertain terms to cut this crap out.

"Well," Eleanor said before clapping her thin lips shut.

She blinked at her daughter as if just seeing her for the first time in forever, and then shook her head.

"I don't know where I went wrong—" she started and then held up a hand when Ava would have said something else. "But you are my only child, and I love you. So I guess we'll work this out. But if you think I'm going to eat from Styrofoam containers, as you just said, our relationship is going to take a bad turn."

Ava grinned. "They have real dishes here, Mother."

Working things out still meant that Eleanor had definite opinions about Ava's life and her career, and it was going to take a little more than delicious lasagna, buttery garlic bread and a great red wine to change that.

"You can still afford a better car than this." Eleanor was fussing as they drove onto the road heading back to the B and B.

The trattoria was located about twenty minutes outside the main part of town, but Ava loved their food, so she made the drive frequently. Only, her trips were usually during daylight hours. As it was a little before nine, it had grown pretty dark, and there weren't any streetlights on dirt roads. She switched on her high beams and tried to tune her mother out.

"And why television? If you're going to be in entertainment, why not go for movies? You'll certainly make more money there. I believe there was a studio executive who hired your father's firm at one point. I can probably look him up when I get home to civilization," Eleanor was saying.

"I don't need you to help me get into movies, Mother. I'm doing exactly what I want to do right now."

If that included holding the steering wheel with a death grip as a crack of thunder sounded and the skies opened up, dropping buckets of rain down around them, then so be it.

"Crap!" she said and switched the windshield wipers on.

"It's awfully dark out here, Ava. I don't like it."

"I know you don't like it, Mother. You've spent the three hours you've been in town telling me how much you don't like it here."

"Well, I don't. And that rude woman who came over to our table. What was her name? Millie something? I mean, really, who names their child Millie, nowadays? And she had on too much lipstick, looking at me as if I had offended her in some way," Eleanor continued.

Her mother had definitely offended Millie, considering she'd told her that she could purchase better wigs at professional salons instead of online. In response, Millie had run her fingers through her natural, but permed, hair as she stood over Eleanor and made a snide remark about Ava and Eleanor being suspicious characters in town. After that, and considering the other times Millie had pushed Ava's buttons, Ava hadn't even bothered to apologize for Eleanor's comments.

"Millie Randall is a special character," Ava was saying before something hit the car's fender.

She kept her grip on the steering wheel, but the car had already spun around and was now going down a slight embankment.

Eleanor screamed from the passenger seat, holding her chest and mumbling something about a heart attack, while Ava tried desperately to press on the brakes and keep them from crashing into the trees ahead. The sounds of her heart thumping wildly and her mother's screeching didn't help, so when the car slammed into something hard and the airbags exploded, knocking Ava back against the seat, she sank blissfully into the darkness.

Gage laughed like he hadn't since he was younger. Since he and his siblings were all together in Pensacola.

They were seated in the room that, according to Harper, would eventually become their formal living room. Right now there were two couches and two recliners positioned on an Aubusson rug around a long coffee table that Harper's cousin Craig had made.

Gray and Morgan sat on one couch, while Gage and Harper had pulled the recliners close to each side of the couch. Gray held his phone out with Gen on FaceTime. Gage had his phone with Gia, Harper had hers with Garrek, and Morgan, who had become fast friends with Gemma, had hers out, as well. This was how they'd had a family get-together after dinner.

"I'd forgotten all about that," Gage said after he'd laughed until his sides hurt.

"Well, I didn't," Gia replied. "All of our dolls were floating in the ocean after you and Garrek decided they could take a cruise on the raft you'd built out of branches and old shoeboxes."

"Gia cried for days," Gemma recalled with a chuckle.

"And Mom punished us for a week because we didn't ask permission to use your dolls on the virgin voyage," Garrek added.

Gray laughed. "I warned you two not to go in their bedroom, but you wouldn't listen."

"Gage was a master manipulator back then," Gen said. "He'd convince you that anything was a good idea. Remember he got Mom to let us open a gift not only on Christmas Eve, but on the day before Christmas Eve, too. Telling her it was a shame that only those two days out of the month got all the attention."

"And I used to cry about being an only child," Harper said, shaking her head.

"Those were good times," Gemma said. "I miss us all being together."

"I've missed it, too," Gage admitted. "But Gray's kids have reminded me of all that."

"Oh yes, I'm sure Jack and Lily have reminded you of how much mischief youngsters can get into," Morgan chimed in.

"More like reminding all of us how important family is," Gray said soberly.

"Speaking of which," Garrek announced and cleared his throat. "The last time we all met, Gray informed us that he'd narrowed down where the money that was deposited into the Grand Cayman account had come from."

"Someone who lived in a group home on Broad Street," Gage added.

He didn't really want to talk about this, but figured it was probably best for them all to decide to leave it alone.

"I've driven past there a few times, and I have to say, I really don't care who lived in that house or who followed Dad's instructions and deposited that money in the account. I've decided to use some of my share to start my own research foundation," Gage said.

He hadn't planned to announce this just yet, but since they were all here—so to speak—now was as good a time as any.

"Really?" Gray asked. "When did you decide this?"

"I've been thinking about it since I arrived in Temptation. My career didn't exactly work out the way I had planned, so I figured it was time for me to regroup and start again," he told them.

He left out the part that included Ava being a big influence on his decision. She'd always known what she wanted to do in life, and she'd even gone against her mother's wishes to achieve her goals. Gage had even told her she was doing the right thing, that she had a right to live the life she wanted. Well, he was making plans to live the life he wanted, with or without Mortimer Gogenheim and the chief of obstetrics position at Nancy Links Medical Center.

"I'm going to use my money to open my own restaurant," Gia announced.

"And I've been thinking about teaching and expanding my company to offer design grants in some of the colleges," Gen added.

"Onward and upward," Gemma told them. "Just like Daddy used to say."

There was a moment of silence, and then Gray spoke.

"I'll dismiss the private investigators, and we'll all accept that Dad left us this additional money because he loved us."

Morgan touched her husband's knee and smiled up at him.

"I agree," Garrek said. "We'll finally begin to focus on our future instead of being bogged down by our past."

"That's a great idea," Harper told her fiancé.

The Taylor sextuplets agreed.

"Now, with that said," Garrek began again, "I hear Gage is settling in to Temptation with a certain young lady who's been visiting, as well."

Oh no, Gage thought as all eyes, even the ones via FaceTime, zeroed in on him.

"Yes!" Morgan exclaimed. "You should see them together. They're so cute. Especially when they babysit the babies. I've used them as sitters twice now, and I would definitely recommend them."

His sister-in-law happily grinned at him, and Gage could only shake his head. He'd grown to love her and the stability and happiness she'd provided for his older brother.

"Ooooh, tell us more," Gia prodded.

Gage dragged his free hand down his face and groaned. "It's no big deal. Her name's Ava, and we worked together on her television show earlier this year. She's in Temptation for a writing retreat."

"Uh-huh, during the same time that Gage decided to come back for a visit and has since decided to stay on longer," Harper added.

"Yes, I came back to see Gray and his family. And I started working on the project Dad wanted at the hospital, so I don't want to leave until it's up and running smoothly," Gage said.

"And she just showed up? At the same time?" Gen asked. "Hmm."

"Right. Hmm," Morgan added.

"It was a coincidence," Gage said, but had to admit the words didn't sound accurate even to his mind.

"A coincidence that one of the famous Taylor sextuplets would be selected to work on another television show. And then that the producer from that show would arrive in our hometown at the exact same time that you did?" Gen asked.

"That's a pretty big coincidence," Gray said.

"Ava didn't know I was coming here," Gage replied calmly. But he was feeling anything but calm at the moment.

Why had they brought this up, and why were they questioning what had been just a chance happening? He had nothing to do with Ava showing up here and neither did his family.

Another phone ringing interrupted the conference, and Harper handed Morgan her cell phone as she stood and crossed the room to answer the landline.

"Morgan, it's Wendy for you," Harper said.

Morgan gave her cell phone to Gray and took the cordless phone from Harper.

"So we're all set for Christmas?" Gemma asked. "Everyone's coming back to Temptation for dinner in the Victorian on Peach Tree Lane?"

She sounded wistful as she smiled, and Gage wanted nothing more than to reach out and hug her. Gemma was the closest to their mother, and Olivia's love and caring nature radiated through his sister. He hadn't realized how much he missed being close to her until this very moment.

"Ava's been in an accident," Morgan said, her words effectively ending the good mood of their family conference.

"What?" Gage asked as he stood, immediately dropping his phone onto the couch.

"Wendy's on duty tonight, and she said they were just brought in by ambulance. A trucker was driving down Chambray Road and saw her car in a ditch," Morgan announced.

"I'm going now," Gage announced and had taken only a couple of steps toward the door before Gray came up behind him.

"I'll go with you. Here, take this," he said and handed Gage his phone that he'd dropped.

Gage didn't know when his other siblings were disconnected from their call, but he was on his way out the door in the next few seconds and heading to his car. All he could think about was Ava at this moment. Was she hurt? What had happened? Would he ever see her again?

Chapter 11

"Is there a possibility that you could be pregnant?"

Gage felt the world around him shift as he paused outside the curtain in the emergency room. It was only partially closed, and he'd been directed this way after he'd asked for Ava. He could see her lying on the bed, the doctor who had just asked the question holding her hand, checking her pulse.

"No," she replied. "I'm on birth control."

And he'd used protection. Each and every time they were together, Gage had dutifully donned a condom. So why had his heart rate significantly increased the moment he heard that question? More importantly, why was he feeling a sting of disappointment at her answer?

"Okay, good. We'll note that on your chart in case

we need to send you for an MRI or CT scan," the doctor continued.

He reached forward and grabbed an otoscope from the shelf on the wall, then proceeded to check Ava's eyes. When he was finished, he used his fingers to check down her neck and her limbs. She lay on the bed, staring up at the ceiling as the exam continued, and Gage resisted the urge to immediately go to her. As a doctor, he knew it was imperative for this physical exam to occur without interruption or distraction. So he remained where he stood, watching every part of the exam and breathing a sigh of relief when the doctor finally said, "I think you have a mild concussion."

"That means I can go home, right?" Ava asked. "I mean, I don't have to be admitted?"

"No. But I'd like someone to be there for you in case your symptoms change. You're just visiting us in Temptation, is that correct?"

"Yes. I'm staying at the Sunnydale Bed-and-Breakfast."

The doctor nodded. "Louisa Reed's place. She's a great innkeeper and would probably watch after you, but I don't think she lives on the property anymore. Moved into a smaller house near her daughter after her son, Harry, went to jail."

"She can come home with me," Gage said, finally entering the room completely. "I'll be able to keep a close eye on her in case her symptoms worsen."

"And you are?" the doctor asked when he spun around to see Gage approaching.

Gage extended his hand and said, "Dr. Gage Taylor."

With a smile and a curt nod, the doctor shook Gage's

hand. "Yes. Talk around the hospital is you were here and taking charge of the new wing your brother just finished building."

"That's correct. I'm in obstetrics and gynecology," Gage told him. "I'll take Ava home when you discharge her."

She'd started to sit up then, and Gage moved closer to the bed, taking her hand.

"And you're staying in that nice pretty yacht down at the dock. She's a beauty. I'm Dr. Ralston Hackney. My wife owns the ice-cream parlor at the end of the dock. She can't stop talking about that yacht. Think I may have to look into buying a boat or something just to keep her quiet."

Gage smiled. "Let me know when you're ready, I've got a great agent who can work wonders with the financing."

"I'll keep that in mind."

"Um, excuse me? Can I go now? I'd like to check on my mother."

"Oh, yes, Ms. Cannon. Sorry about that. I'll get started on your discharge papers. Dr. Taylor here will know what to watch for, but the nurse will go over everything when she comes in with the paperwork. Also, your mother's been taken down to X-ray. Dr. Leon Schilling in orthopedics examined her and thinks she broke her ankle. He's not talking about surgery, so she may be put in a cast and ready to leave in a few hours."

Ava sighed. "Just great."

"You're both very lucky the airbags deployed, Ms. Cannon. From what the paramedics said when they brought you in, that little compact car of yours is a total loss," Dr. Hackney said.

"It was a rental," Ava said and closed her eyes.

"Well, then, that's the rental company's problem," Dr. Hackney continued with a grin. "I'll go get your paperwork started. Take care of her, Dr. Taylor."

"Please, call me Gage, and yes, I will take care of her," Gage said and waited until Hackney was out of the room before he turned his attention back to Ava.

Her hair was splayed over the pillow behind her. The T-shirt she wore was wrinkled but not torn or splotched with any blood. Her legs looked good, ankles straight, feet still wearing flat shoes. Everything looked just fine, he concluded after he completed his own visual assessment. Everything except her eyes were closed tight and her fingers trembled in his.

For the first time since Morgan told him about the accident, Gage breathed in slow, measured intervals. Relief eased over him, and he leaned down, kissing Ava's forehead.

"You scared the life out of me," he whispered. "I didn't know what I was going to find once I got here. And I'm pretty sure at least six people are going to report me to the sheriff for speeding through town."

"It was a deer," she said quietly, her eyes opening as he pulled back slightly. "It was so dark and then it started to rain. My mother was complaining, and I just wanted to hurry up and get back to the B and B so I could get her a room of her own and I could find some peace and quiet."

Her voice cracked at the end.

"I wanted her to shut up. She hates it here, and Millie didn't make that situation any better. But I just wanted her to be quiet, or to not be here and now..." Her words trailed off.

"Now, she's going to get her ankle fixed up and spend a few more days here with you," he said and squeezed her hand. "She's fine, Ava. She's going to recover just like you will."

"The car."

"It's a rental. They're insured. And if they're not, I'll pay for the damn car," he said.

She started to shake her head, and Gage saw the moment pain radiated through her with the action.

"Shhhh, baby. Don't move. Don't think about any of this right now. I'm gonna take you home and get you into bed. You'll feel better after you get some rest."

"Home," she said when she opened her eyes again and stared up at him. "Everybody keeps saying 'when I go home.' But I live in LA."

"Logistics," Gage said. "I own a condo in New York, so that's technically my home. But for the last couple of weeks, since we've been staying on my yacht, that's felt more like a home to me than any place I've been since I was a child."

It was true, as the warmth spreading throughout his body and the intense weight he felt in his chest at this very moment indicated. Gage lifted her hand up to his lips and kissed her fingers. He closed his eyes, and words he'd been thinking the last couple of days came tumbling out.

"I haven't trusted any relationship since I was kid,

Ava. Once my dad left, I started to feel like a relationship between a man and woman could never work. Someone was bound to stop caring, or loving enough, and then it would be over."

He stared down at her, into her brown eyes. With his free hand he traced the line of her jaw, before brushing his knuckles over her cheek.

"Then when I was in the sixth grade and had just started middle school, I met these two guys, Fredro and Kelvin." He gave a wry chuckle. "I thought I was finally going to have friends who weren't my brothers. Gray was on the basketball team and Garrek had joined the Boy Scouts. I hadn't yet found my niche, that's what my mom said. Fredro and Kelvin just seemed to have so much fun. Laughing and joking all the time in the cafeteria, in class and on the bus. So when they invited me to go to the park with them one day I thought, This is great! I'll be doing something without my siblings. Because, you know it's hard sometimes being part of a group."

Gage took another deep breath.

"It was a cool friendship for about a week, and then Fredro asked if they could come to my house. I asked my mom and she said it was fine. That Saturday afternoon they came over. The next thing I know they're in my room, going through my stuff saying what they'd like to have. Fredro wanted my baseball bat and glove because it was signed by Eddie Murray. My dad had given it to me for my last birthday. Kelvin wanted the Lakers jersey my mom had given me for Christmas. I told them they couldn't have it. And Fredro looked me right in the eye and said, 'You think you're too good to share your stuff. Just because your family's famous doesn't make you better than us.' I couldn't believe it."

"Gage," she whispered.

He shook his head.

"I told them to put my stuff down and leave, but Fredro refused. So I punched him, and when he fell back on the bed, I took my stuff from him. He charged me and we fought. Kelvin would have jumped in, but Gray heard the noise and he came into the room. Kelvin didn't move and Gray let us fight. At least until my mom came in. Fredro's and Kelvin's mothers called our house later that day, and I heard my mother telling them to teach their kids some manners and they wouldn't end up in fights. Gray and Garrek told me not to worry about it. And on Monday when I went to school, I was prepared for round two. What I wasn't prepared for was the way everybody stared at me in class that day. Nobody talked to me or even wanted to look at me. Not that day or the days that followed. I was an outcast, again. Just because I was born a Taylor sextuplet.

"I vowed to never trust any type of relationship—"

Gage paused, trying to process the things going through his mind at this moment, the memories and the pain.

He lowered his forehead to rest on hers and closed his eyes. "I could have lost you tonight."

"I'm fine, Gage. Really I am," she whispered.

"But it could have been different. Without those air-bags…if you hadn't been able to slow your descent…it could have ended differently."

She'd lifted her other hand to rub down the back of his head. "But it didn't and I'm going to be fine. I'm still right here with you."

His eyes opened at her words, and he pulled back just a little until he could hold her gaze once more.

"With me," he said. "That's where I want you to be. Stay on the yacht with me."

Gage didn't know what he expected, but tears definitely weren't on the list. Of course, he'd never done this before, but he didn't think that asking a woman that he was sleeping with to stay with him on his yacht, instead of at a B and B, was such a bad idea.

"What's the matter, sweetness? Are you in pain?"

She shook her head quickly, an act that Gage knew had to cause her some pain, if she wasn't already experiencing it. He immediately cupped her face with his hands to keep her still, the warmth of her tears touching his palms.

"No. I mean, a little. But I just… I should say so many things to you first, Gage."

"Nonsense," he said. "All you need to say is yes, and I'll take care of everything else."

She waited for what felt like the longest moment in his life before blinking more tears, and replying, "Yes."

"This isn't a hotel, but the decor is impeccable," Eleanor said after Morgan and Harper had gotten her situated on the half tester bed.

"Thank you so much for letting her stay here," Ava said as she came to stand beside Harper. "I'll hire a full-time nurse to look after her until she's well enough to travel. And I'll come by every day to make sure she's not harassing you or any of your staff."

Harper touched Ava's shoulder. "It's fine, Ava. Dr. Schilling gave us plenty of pain meds. Not that we plan to overdose her or anything."

Ava shook her head and managed a smile. "Believe me, you're gonna want to."

"We'll all pitch in and help keep watch over her. They said it was a clean break, but Wendy said with her age, any number of complications could arise if she doesn't heal properly," Morgan told her.

Ava sighed. "I don't know how to thank you two. I mean, you hardly know me and you all showed up at the hospital, and you're so willing to help."

"That's what families do," Morgan said as she moved to put an arm around Ava's shoulders.

"She's right," Harper added. "Now, you should really get some rest yourself. A mild concussion is nothing to play with."

Ava did have a headache, but she feared it had nothing to do with the car accident. She wasn't in a hurry to go back to the yacht with Gage. He was going to undress her and put her to bed, and then he was going to lie beside her and cuddle her in his arms.

And while all that sounded just fine, the real reason for her headache was because she was a big liar, and she had been deceiving him and his family for two months.

"Yes," she admitted. "I am really tired."

They left her alone with her mother, who was already dozing off as a result of the strong pain medication Dr. Schilling had prescribed for her. Ava took a moment to look down at her mother and then to think on everything Gage had said to her just a few hours ago.

It was time to stop letting the past dictate her future. If her mother couldn't do that, it was her decision. Ava was only going to focus on moving forward.

"Good night, Mother," Ava said as she leaned over and kissed Eleanor's cheek. "I'll see you in the morning."

With that she left the room, walking down the grand staircase in Harper's gorgeous home. It was another one of those movie-like romance scenes as she descended the stairs and Gage stood at the bottom looking up at her, waiting for her.

Each step Ava took grew heavier as she realized what she now stood to lose because of the sacrifice she'd decided to make for her career.

"Ready to go?" Gage asked her.

Ava nodded, words clogged in her throat because she knew which ones she needed to speak, but couldn't bring herself to do it. Not yet. Not tonight. Her head was still throbbing, and her body had begun to ache. Gage had asked her to stay with him, which was a huge step for both of them. It had been an eventful enough night. Waiting a few more hours to tell Gage about her plans wasn't too much to ask.

Still, by the time they'd arrived at the yacht, the weight on her chest had become too much to bear, and as soon as they'd entered his bedroom she opened her mouth to speak. Gage, however, lifted a finger to touch her lips.

"A warm shower, a pain pill and rest. That's what I'm prescribing for you," he said.

"Gage, I need to tell you—" she tried to say.

"Not tonight," he interrupted. "Let me just take care of you tonight."

It was so easy to give him what he wanted. So blissfully intimate standing in the shower stall while Gage lathered the sponge and bathed her. So peaceful lying in the bed cuddled in his arms.

"I can't wait for you to meet my sisters," he whispered as Ava began to doze off. "I hope you'll be able to arrange your schedule to be here for Christmas."

"I want to be here for Christmas," Ava said, her eyelids too heavy to hold open any longer.

She'd been chilly once she stepped out of the shower, but now, with his arm wrapped around her and his body cocooning hers, she felt warm and safe. And loved. She really liked those feelings.

"And I've decided to resign from the hospital in New York. I'm going to open my own clinic and research foundation. All Saints cannot provide funding for parents who cannot afford fertility treatments, or certain aspects of taking care of multiple infants. I want to start some programs that will help," he was saying.

Ava's lips lifted in a smile. Gage had stopped her from talking, but he clearly had lots to say tonight. She snuggled closer to him, loving the sound of his voice and thinking of how it would be to do this every night with him. To lie in bed and discuss their goals and dreams, the future they would share. She wanted that. Ava wanted it so very much.

So before she drifted off and while Gage was still talking, she said a little prayer, asking a big favor. *Please let him understand.*

Chapter 12

Ava rolled over and reached for him, but felt the cool sheets instead. Cracking an eye open, she saw the pillows still indented from where he'd laid his head throughout the night. She rolled over again, this time plopping onto her back and then groaning at the slight thumping in her temples.

Dropping an arm over her forehead, she sighed and thought about Gage holding her in his arms last night. It was a magical feeling, one she knew now that she wanted to feel every night of her life. With that thought, Ava sat up slowly. There was no nausea and no dizziness, just the mild headache. Encouraged by the minimal symptoms, she got out of the bed and headed toward the bathroom. The note was taped to the door, and she smiled as she read his words.

I knew you wouldn't stay in bed as per doctor's orders. Gray needed my help with festival setup so Morgan's taking the morning shift with you while Harper stays with your mom. In the afternoon, Harper's going to come over. If you're doing well, Harper will bring you to the festival in time for the pumpkin-carving contest. If you have any symptoms you are to stay in bed, or at the very least, on the yacht and I'll hurry with the contest and come back to you. Gage

After a warm shower, Ava dressed in jeans and a button-front plaid shirt and slipped her feet into slippers that she knew had been at the B and B. Someone must have gone there and brought her things here because as she looked around the room, she also saw her bag, laptop and the toiletries she'd had on the dresser there, now sitting on top of the second dresser here.

It was different seeing her perfume bottles sitting next to Gage's cologne, her laptop on the table near the door with his right across from it. She turned back and looked again at the rumpled bed where they'd slept and sighed. If she wanted this lovely scene to be a part of her future, she had to set things in motion.

Morgan was on morning duty, so that meant she was probably above deck in one of the lavish rooms up there, waiting for Ava to emerge. Finding her phone on the charger sitting on the nightstand, she picked it up and moved to the table. Taking a seat, she booted up her laptop and called Marcelle.

"Hi there! I know it's early, but I really need to talk

to you about something," Ava began the moment she heard the groggy "hello" on the other end.

Marcelle was not a morning person, so calling her at seven thirty LA time would normally be a no-no. In this case, it was urgent, so Ava ignored the time.

"This better be good, Ava," Marcelle replied.

"I think it is," she said. "I'm sending you an email right now. I need you to review the two attachments. There's a synopsis of the two-night miniseries featuring the Taylors of Temptation and notes on how this deal has to be brokered."

"Has to be?" Marcelle asked, her voice a little clearer now.

Ava had known that business would wake Marcelle up completely. It always did.

"Yes," Ava told her. "Because this is how I'm going to pitch the story to the Taylors, and I'm pretty certain if I pitch it this way, and they agree, they're not going to take kindly to any abrupt changes."

"I take it this is different from what Jenner and Carroll told me about when they called me last week."

Ava's fingers stilled over the keyboard, and she had to readjust the phone she'd tucked between her ear and shoulder. She probably should have hunted through her purse to find her Bluetooth, but she hadn't wanted to waste any more time.

"They called you? Why?" she asked Marcelle.

There was some rattling in the phone's background, and Ava figured Marcelle had climbed out of bed and was now heading toward her home office so she could boot up her computer and read the email while they talked.

"They were pretty excited about this show and wanted to get started on getting you signed on officially."

"Well, you might want to hold off on that," Ava told her. "Because if they don't agree, I'm walking."

"Really?" Marcelle asked, her voice clear and questioning. "What about your new show idea?"

"I'm not going to be bullied by them," Ava said, wondering why she hadn't taken this stance from the start.

Fear. That was the clear-cut reason. She was afraid that going against top network executives would get her blackballed in the industry. And there was still a chance of that happening. Only now, she didn't give a damn. If she had to use her trust fund money to make her own movies, or buy a network where she could decide which shows would make it and which ones wouldn't, that's what she planned to do. Asking for and waiting for permission or validation from pompous men in this industry was over.

Gage had told her that. He'd said she shouldn't apologize for who and what she was to her mother and that she was enough on her own. Ava believed him because he believed in her.

Marcelle gave a whoop and said, "That's what I've been waiting to hear from you. Okay, let me look at the notes first because I already know your pitch is awesome."

"I don't want their lives intruded upon for months on end. The four-hour series can be taped in a month, edited the next month, advertised and shown in the same timespan they already have mapped out. But making this a full thirteen-week series is out of the question. They have lives and families and it's just too much to ask them to go through all of this again," Ava said.

"Okay, this all looks good. I'll work on your numbers. You're doing them a huge favor, and in return they're going to pay you a big damn chunk of money. And I want a clause in this contract that guarantees your next two shows. And…hmm, wait a minute," Marcelle said.

Ava was going through her email inbox seeing what she needed to read and what could be trashed, so she didn't speak while Marcelle paused.

"Well, this is very interesting indeed," Marcelle said after another minute or so.

"What's that?" Ava asked, just as she was about to close her email in-box. She needed to get topside to let Morgan know she was all right; otherwise Morgan might come down to check on her. Ava didn't want to be seen working when she was supposed to be recuperating.

"Apparently I need to check my office voice mail quicker. Parker Donovan sent an email to follow up to the message he left for me yesterday. He's very interested in meeting with you and discussing creative opportunities for you at Donovan Network Television," Marcelle told her.

Ava sat back in the chair and smiled. She couldn't help it—a fist bump in the air also came as she did everything she could to withhold the squeal of excitement that bubbled inside her.

"Yes!" she exclaimed. "So Jenner and Carroll can definitely take this deal for the Taylors or kick rocks!"

"You're damn right!" Marcelle yipped, excitement clear in her voice, as well. "Okay, since they're on the East Coast like you right now, I'll give them a call to let them know that I've received the message and I'm checking your availability. I'll also get a preliminary idea of what these Donovans are possibly talking about offering you to come to their network."

"Great. Keep me posted," Ava said. "Now, I've gotta go. Today's the Fall Festival."

Marcelle chuckled. "You're really settling into that little town, aren't you?"

Ava shrugged even though she knew Marcelle couldn't see her. "It happened so naturally. I mean, one minute I'll be sitting in my room writing and the next Otis is knocking on my door with the best home-made lemonade I've ever had and some sort of snack. While I eat, he tells me whatever is going on in town for that day. Then I go outside and people stop me on the street to talk about this or that. And the Taylors, they're super nice and very involved and—I guess I am getting caught up, huh?"

Marcelle chuckled. "Definitely. But Gage Taylor is scrumptious enough to have any woman moving to a small town and going to fall festivals, whatever those are."

Ava agreed and ended the call with Marcelle. She had just stood from the desk when she heard the door to the room open and Morgan come down. Just in time, she thought and then fixed a smile on her face to greet one of the nicest women she'd ever known. A woman who she could easily picture as a sister-in-law someday.

Gage could not ignore the instant swell of happiness that spread throughout his chest the moment he saw Ava come through the double doors of the old Hatlenbinger horse barn. It was chilly today, so she wore jeans, those sexy brown boots that tied up the back of her legs and a brown leather jacket. Her hair was styled in two braids, each hanging over one shoulder so that she looked younger and prettier. She stood still for a few moments, looking around the large structure similar to the way Gage had when he'd first entered a few hours ago to help Gray and the others set up.

The barn used to house Hatlenbinger's prized stallions and foaling mares when Gage had been younger. But, as told to him earlier by Fred Randall, Tom Hatlenbinger died of a massive heart attack ten years ago. After an argument with his two daughters prior to his death, he'd left everything he had to his second wife, who in turn sold the horses within the same month that Tom had passed away. The land had been bought by the town for taxes a few years prior to Tom's death, so his wife couldn't sell that, and the town decided to use the barn space to host the weekly farmer's market. The house had been renovated and was being used as a horse museum thanks to one of Hatlenbinger's daughters, who had returned to town.

Today it was filled with booths showcasing home-made items for sale. They had everything from jams to baskets to knitted sweaters. There were also tables crowded with cakes and pies, cookies and smoked meats for tasting and sale. In one of the far corners were bales of hay and a tractor for picture-taking and playing, as some children were already doing. Next to that section were five tables and an insane amount of pumpkins all ready for the contest.

"You just gonna stare at her for the rest of the day?" Gray asked.

Gage hadn't heard his brother approach and didn't bother to look over at him because he knew the smirk that would be on his face.

"She's mingling," he replied.

Two women Gage did not know had just stopped to speak to Ava, and he watched the exchange in awe of how quickly she'd made friends in this town.

"And you're ogling," Gray said. "You're so pitiful."

"Hey," Gage replied and then tore his gaze away from Ava long enough to glare at Gray. "No name-calling is allowed when you came here to sell three pieces of property and ended up marrying a woman, getting her pregnant and adopting her children."

Gray didn't look the least bit bothered by Gage's words, but instead shook his head. "You're not me," he said with a slow grin.

"Whatever, man. I'm not ashamed to admit that I came here for a visit and ended up falling in love."

"That's cool, because denying it would have been foolish. It's written all over your face," Gray said. "And truthfully, it looks good on you. I'm happy for you, especially considering how you both came to be here."

Gage did not want to hear about that coincidence again. He'd been thinking about it off and on since his siblings brought it up last night. It wasn't on purpose, he'd told himself finally, and that was that.

"To be fair, we hooked up after the end of shooting the first season of the show," he told Gray.

It wasn't something Gage would have normally told anyone, but he was tired of them acting as if he and Ava were only connected because they ended up in Temptation together.

"Really? Sleeping with the boss?" Gray said and folded his arms over his chest.

"Nah, it wasn't like that. There was this chemistry between us from day one. We fought it the whole time we were working, but then once the shooting was over, I guess we just figured it was fair to proceed." Gage thought back fondly on that night in Ava's trailer. "It was only supposed to be one time."

"But then she showed up here," Gray said.

Gage nodded. "And we were at it again. But this time it was different. I knew one more time wasn't going to be enough."

"It never is when you find the one." Gray clapped Gage on the shoulder. "Like I said, I'm happy for you. Ava's a good woman. Morgan and Harper love her, so all you have to do is get Gen's, Gemma's and Gia's approval, and you can go ahead and propose to her."

"Propose? I don't know if I'm ready to start thinking about marriage."

Gray chuckled. "Yeah, you keep right on telling yourself that."

"Really, I wasn't."

"Uh-huh. Well, if you aren't thinking about putting a ring on it, you probably should," Gray told him and then pointed toward the door once more.

Gage followed his brother's direction and saw Ava laughing at something Craig Presley was saying. More importantly, he saw how close Ava and Craig were standing to each other and how Ava easily rested her hand on Craig's arm.

He took a step in their direction and heard Gray laugh.

"Yeah, that's what I thought," his brother was saying, but Gage kept walking, until he came up behind Ava and Craig.

It was just in time to hear Ava say, "I'm sorry I never followed through on the rain check for dinner. I had work and then things just started happening."

Craig smiled down at her. "Yeah, things like you and Gage hooking up. I get it, and there are no worries. I was just offering to show you around."

"And I appreciate it," Ava said. "You were very friendly and helpful when I first arrived."

"Hey there," Gage said when he finally stepped up to them. "You look like you're feeling better."

"Hey. I am," she said and then looked up at him as if nobody else in that barn even existed.

"How's it going, Craig?" Gage spoke and extended his hand to shake the younger man's.

"Hey, Gage. Going great. Been pretty busy with projects, but Harper said we'll slow down for the holidays. We're still waiting on Ava to decide when and where she wants to build her tiny house, though," Craig said.

"I haven't even had a moment to think about that lately," Ava said.

"Well, you should," Craig continued. "Temptation's a great place to have a small getaway home."

Gage agreed. "You don't have much time to think about it now either. We're up," he told her. "The contest is about to start."

"Oh, right. See ya later, Craig," Ava said as Gage took her hand.

"What do you mean, 'see ya later'? I'm entered in the contest, so be prepared to be wowed by my creation!"

As they walked across the barn to the area set up for the contest, Gage couldn't help but think about Craig's words to Ava. Temptation was a great place to build a house. But what else? A family? A home?

An hour and a half later, Ava hugged Craig and placed the goofy jack-o'-lantern sponge hat on his head. He was the winner of the pumpkin-carving contest, and as such had won the lovely hat and a fifty-dollar coupon to O'Reiley's Pumpkin Patch. His pumpkin-turned-Darth-Vader was the best carving Ava and Gage had ever seen.

Gray, Jack and Lily came in second place and had posed happily with their creation—a crooked but valiant attempt at the Grinch. The contest had been a blast. The hot cider and sugar cookies being passed around were even better. But overall, it was just the people,

Ava thought, that made this a fantastic event. She'd been to who knew how many Hollywood parties and corporate functions with her mother, but none of them compared to this.

"It's movie time!" Jack yelled excitedly.

Morgan was there shaking her head. "I don't know. I heard Craig telling Harper that he picked something extra scary for tonight's movie. I don't think you and your sister will be able to watch."

Harper waved a hand. "My aunt Laura quickly put the kibosh on that," she said. "We're watching *It's The Great Pumpkin, Charlie Brown* first, and then Craig's allowed to show *Poltergeist*, but not the other horribly gruesome movie he was planning on."

"Charlie Brown! I love Charlie Brown!" Lily announced.

"Okay, then let's head on out so we can get a good seat in front of the screen," Morgan told them.

"We're just going to clean up here a little. Save us a seat," Ava told Morgan and Gray.

"Oh no, you're not," Gage warned. "You're going to go on and sit down. I'll clean up, and then I'll join you. So you can save me a seat."

When Ava opened her mouth to argue, Wendy, Morgan's sister, touched her shoulder. "Don't even bother. Take the offer of help 'cause who knows when you'll get another one."

Ava liked Wendy because she reminded her so much of Marcelle. She agreed with her, and they all walked outside to where chairs had been set up in rows on the grass like they were at a real movie theatre. A large screen had been rented and placed up front for the movie viewing. They found seats in the fourth row, and Ava eased down the aisle to sit alongside the Taylor family.

It felt perfect sitting here, waiting for the movie to begin, talking to Lily, stopping Jack from climbing over the chairs in the next row and laughing with Wendy and Harper. She'd never had moments like this with her mother, or even with both her parents when her father was alive. This was what it was like to belong to a real family. She smiled to herself and thanked every deity possible for her good fortune.

"Attention! Attention!" A woman stood in front of the screen with a microphone.

Ava recalled meeting her before. She was one of the women who had been with Millie the second time the brash woman had approached her. Her name was Shirley Hampstead, and she was the town comptroller. Ava loved putting names with faces and job titles. It was a lot better than putting names with the last movie someone had done, or the last scandal they'd been involved in. She put a finger up to her lips and gave Jack a stern look before returning her attention to Shirley.

"We'd like to thank everyone for coming out to this year's festival. It's been a wonderful day, and we owe it all to the Magnolia Guild for their fund-raisers throughout the year that help us pay for events like this." Shirley gave a nod to someone in the audience, and there was applause.

"Also, on behalf of Mayor Pullum, who's still recovering from knee surgery, we want to thank all of this year's volunteers. Without you we wouldn't have been set up on time." With that, Shirley and a few other people in the audience laughed and clapped.

"As always, a very special thanks goes to JoEllen Camby for planning this function—from her house—every single year. JoEllen does a magnificent job," Shirley told the crowd, who clapped in response.

Wendy leaned over to whisper to Ava. "And that, my dear, is how you serve sarcasm here in Temptation."

Ava laughed and shook her head.

Then her smile faltered slightly as a familiar face joined Shirley. Millie wore a burnt-orange pantsuit with a white blouse and a large pumpkin pendant on the lapel of her jacket.

"Now, I've saved the best for last," Shirley said. "I'm so excited about this announcement, I could just bust."

Shirley did a little shake that may have been meant to accompany her words about busting, but actually made her look a little insane, as she wore a tight green dress that surely would not support her body parts in the event any busting were to actually take place. Millie snatched the microphone from Shirley before anything like that could happen.

"As the chairperson of Temptation's chamber of commerce, I'll be making the next announcement," Millie started to say.

Ava looked around for Gage at that moment because she really didn't want to hear anything that Millie had to say. The woman was a troublemaker, and she was rude and annoying.

"This time last year, we welcomed back to town a

member of one of our most esteemed families. I'd like to ask Grayson Taylor and his wife and children to stand," Millie said.

Harper leaned over in her seat, looking past Ava to where Wendy sat. Wendy shrugged and Harper shook her head. Ava watched as Gray stood with Jack on his shoulders and Morgan stood with Lily standing in the seat beside her. The audience clapped once again.

"Yes, welcome back to the Taylors," Millie continued. "I'm saying that with a plural because Garrek Taylor was back with us for a few months this year. Just long enough to snag the heart of our very own Harper Presley. Harper, you come on and stand, too."

Harper groaned as she got to her feet, and Ava gave her a conciliatory pat on her back when she sat down again.

"It seems like all the Taylors are coming home," Millie went on to say. "And with that comes our big announcement. As you all know, once upon a time *The Taylors of Temptation* was a reality show. And this show brought lots of revenue to our fair town. Now, thirty years later when reality television is still going strong, the Taylors are going to help our town out once again by filming an all-new reality show."

Ava's heart sank, and her throat went dry as whispers began to sound in the audience.

"That's right, the new show is going to be called *The Taylors of Temptation: Remember the Times*. And it's all set to air this time next year. Filming will start soon after the first of the year, so in addition to welcoming the rest of the Taylor sextuplets home, we'll also be preparing for visitors. The crew and all those Hollywood folk will be staying here in town and eating and shopping. We'll make enough money to fix the bridge down by the stream and make necessary improvements to the dock, as well as help some of the local businesses refresh their storefronts. We want to look our best, of course."

All of a sudden Ava didn't know what to do with her hands. They'd been resting in her lap, but now she was wringing them, and when she realized what she was doing she hurriedly dropped them to her sides. She didn't want to look to her left or to her right, because Wendy and Harper were most likely staring at her in question. Instead she looked over the heads of the audience toward the barn, where Gage now stood, his gaze zeroing in on her.

"So let's give a great big round of applause to the Hollywood producer Ava Cannon, who has been staying with us these past couple of months. Ava's been here scouting locations and getting the Taylor family ready to be in the spotlight once again. Come on and stand up so we can all see you, Ava."

Ava didn't stand. She didn't need to. All eyes were immediately on her. But the only ones she gave a damn about were his.

Chapter 13

Gage gripped the steering wheel as he drove them toward the dock. So many things had been flowing through his mind since they'd left the festival, but he knew he'd needed to take a moment to get his thoughts together.

"Is that what this has been about?" Gage asked when he stopped his car.

After Millie's announcement he'd stood still, unable to move a muscle as he watched Ava moving through the crowd toward him. She was trying to get out of the row where she'd been sitting, but people kept congratulating her, or simply standing just to shake her hand. To shake the hand of the producer of the new Taylors of Temptation reality show.

"No," she immediately replied. "We… What we have is separate."

"Separate from you brokering a deal for a show that was never going to happen," he replied.

His hands slipped slowly off the steering wheel to rest in his lap. He felt calm, dangerously so.

"The deal happened before us, or rather, before this 'us' began," she said and then turned sideways in the seat to look at him. "Let me just explain from the beginning."

Gage shook his head. "You followed me here and weaseled your way into my family, so that you could film us again. You knew how I felt about that show and being in the spotlight from day one, and you stayed, you continued. You lied to me. You used me and my family."

"That's not entirely true," she continued. "When I was approached about this deal, all I knew was that your family had stayed out of the limelight for the last thirty years. I didn't know why."

"And you didn't bother to ask," he responded and felt his entire body begin to shake.

"I wanted a chance to get to know you and the family first, and then I was going to—"

"You were going to what, Ava? Would you have married me if I asked? Had my kids maybe? All to get your precious show. What's the matter, one successful show wasn't enough? Or was it that you couldn't stand your own dysfunctional family so you decided to squirm your way into another one to see if you could destroy it, too?"

She jerked as if he'd physically assaulted her, and Gage frowned.

"I can explain," she said slowly. "I can tell you exactly how this came about and the terms I've requested for you and your family."

"I don't give a damn about any terms," he said, this time through clenched teeth because the calm he'd possessed was slowly slipping. "I don't care about your explanations. This business ruined my family once, there's no way I'm going to let that happen again."

"Gage—" she started.

"No!" he yelled. "I drove you back here so you can get your things. I'll call you a cab while you pack."

He opened the door and stepped out of the car. He closed the door but still stood beside it waiting…for what, he had no idea. To wake up possibly, from this horrid dream. For her to tell him that Millie had lied and none of this was happening. That the woman he'd fallen in love with hadn't screwed him just to see her name roll in the credits of another television show.

He heard the passenger side door open and close softly.

"I apologize for not telling you sooner," she said. "I should have. I knew it all along, and I didn't say anything. I guess I didn't want to destroy the perfect moments we were having."

"They weren't perfect," he replied and gazed at her over the top of the car. "They were lies. All of this was a lie. Just like the show that was on television thirty years ago. We were never that happy family enjoying the limelight. My father was never the happily married man madly in love with his wife. We're not on television right now, so if in your mind this was going to end with a big wedding, a house and kids, you were wrong."

"If you would just let me explain," she tried once more.

"Explain what? That you were just fine sleeping with me and dragging me to parties, but when it really came down to it, you didn't give a damn about me or my feelings."

He took a breath, but more words came, and Gage was helpless to stop them.

"You want to explain why you lay in bed with me every night and never once bothered to tell me you were having my baby? Why did I have to find out the day after you aborted my child when the clinic called to check on you because your blood pressure was running high when you were discharged? Why are you constantly lying and deceiving me when I've told you how hard it was for me to trust anyone?"

Silence fell between them after those last words. Ava stared at him with tears and confusion in her eyes.

Gage cursed.

He ran his hands down his face and cursed again.

"Gage," she gasped.

"No," he said. "Just no. It's enough."

"I didn't know. I'm not like whoever she was. Let me—"

"No!" he yelled. And then sighed. "Just stay the hell away from me."

When she didn't move or speak, he walked around the car to stand directly in front of her.

"I mean it. Get yourself another consultant for your

show and find another family to exploit, because it won't be me or the Taylors. Stay away from me and my family."

He walked away then, letting himself onto the yacht but going straight back to the lounge room, where there was a bar. He needed a drink. And he needed her off his boat and out of his life…before he could deal with the fact that his heart was breaking once again—and this time it had nothing to do with a television show.

It was her fault.

She shouldn't be irritated as hell with Gage. But she was.

How dare he order her to get her stuff off his yacht and then call her a cab to get her away from him as fast as possible? And on top of all that, he'd warned her to stay away from him and his family, as if she had no choice but to listen to him on this matter. There were five other adults involved in this situation—whether she'd talked to all of them directly or not—and they each deserved the opportunity to listen to her proposal and provide an answer. She should just set up a meeting with them and see what happened.

But doing so would hurt him more.

More than what this woman had apparently done to him. He'd had a child, and she took it from him without even telling him. It was no wonder Gage didn't trust people. And Ava had lied to him, as well. She couldn't deny that fact.

Pressing this issue, forcing his family into the spotlight—with or without him—would seal Gage's distrust box closed tightly forever. And even if he couldn't bring himself to stay with her, he deserved love and happiness with someone.

By the time Ava climbed out of the cab, it was almost midnight.

She walked around to the trunk, where the driver was removing her bags. "Here you go." She extended the twenty dollars to him and bent down to pick up the duffel bag he'd placed on the curb.

"Fare's already taken care of," he told her. "I'll carry these others to the door for you."

Ava frowned. What kind of guy put a woman out and paid for her cab fare?

The kind she was desperately in love with.

She knocked on the door, the last bits of her pride in her back pocket, and waited. Harper opened the door and offered her a small smile. A genuine smile.

Once she and all her stuff were in Harper's foyer, Ava cleared her throat and said, "I apologize. I should have been up-front with everyone the moment I interrupted the volleyball game that day."

"You could have done that," Harper said as she folded her arms over her chest. "But then you wouldn't have learned all you did about the Taylor family, and you wouldn't have had the chance to fall in love with Temptation and Gage."

Ava ran her hands through her hair and sighed. "I don't know how any of that happened. I was just trying to do my job."

"But something else occurred," Harper said with a nod. "Been there. Done that."

"You deceived and alienated a family that you not only needed for work, but loved and admired, as well?" Ava asked and chuckled to keep from crying.

"Not exactly," Harper replied. "But it took me a minute to accept the love that had blossomed because of my independence and everything I'd built my life to be."

"There's nothing to accept now," Ava said quietly. "Absolutely nothing."

She walked away from Harper and up that gorgeous romantic stairway with heavy steps. It was all over. Tomorrow she would arrange for her and her mother to go back to LA.

"Oh, Ava. Darling, I wasn't expecting you," Eleanor said and then giggled.

Yes, Ava thought with a start as her eyes widened and her mouth gaped, her mother was giggling. And she was sitting up in the bed accepting grapes from Otis, who sat on the side of the bed, also giggling.

"Ah, hiya, Miss Ava," Otis said before popping another fat grape into her mother's mouth.

"What. Is. Going on here?" Ava asked. She couldn't stop her feet from leading her deeper into the room. Even though her eyes were burning at the sight of her mother in such an—for lack of a better word—intimate position with a man.

"Otis took off work today. He's been here taking care of me since this afternoon when Harper left to go see about you," Eleanor said. "Did you have fun at the festival?"

"No," Ava replied instantly. "That's what I came to talk to you about."

"Well, go ahead and talk," Eleanor told her. "Otis has been such a doll, making sure I had everything I need while recuperating."

"Right," Otis said. He looked from Ava to Eleanor and then back to Ava. "But I think I'll be going now."

"Thank you," Ava said. Since her mother apparently wasn't getting the hint that she needed to talk.

"I'll come check on you tomorrow," Otis said as he stood. He set the bowl of grapes on the nightstand and was about to walk away when Eleanor reached for his hand.

"That's very nice of you, Otis."

"We won't be here tomorrow," Ava said. "I mean, I'll be making arrangements for us to fly out tomorrow."

"We are?" Eleanor asked, the surprised look on her face real and perplexing.

"Oh. Well, yeah, I'll just be going. I, um, guess I'll give you a call or something sometime, Ellie."

Ellie?

Otis touched her mother's hand, and the two shared a look. It wasn't a look that Ava wanted to explore, and so she glanced away from them. Seconds later Otis was touching her shoulder lightly as he walked past.

"It was a pleasure, Miss Ava," he mumbled before leaving the room.

Once the door was closed, Ava moved closer to the bed. "What was that?"

"That was me having the most fun I've had in the last ten years," Eleanor quipped.

Her words, in addition to the situation, once again startled Ava, who sighed and sat on the end of the bed.

"Well, I messed up big-time. So the fun for both of us is over," she said.

"You? The one who has her life together, who knows what she wants and is going to go get it with or without her mother's approval. *You* messed up?"

Her mother was a lot of things, and condescending was one of her specialties. Ava very rarely admitted that Eleanor was right.

"I thought I was doing the right thing," Ava said after recounting the whole story for her mother. "I figured if I could just rework the deal, the Taylors would definitely go for it. And I was going to tell them everything tomorrow night at dinner. I had it all planned out."

"Yes, you seem to plan things out very well," Eleanor said. "The problem is, you don't account for life happening throughout your plan."

Ava kicked off her shoes and turned around, pulling her legs up onto the bed. "What are you talking about?"

Eleanor waved her hand and then fluffed the pillows behind her before settling back again. "Life, Ava. It happens to all of us. Do you think I wanted my successful and handsome husband to turn into an alcoholic? Did I want to have the managing partner of the firm call me and tell me that if my husband didn't get himself together, he would be fired and we would be thrust into the poorhouse?"

The last was a bit dramatic considering Eleanor and Ava had huge trust funds courtesy of Eleanor's godfather, who died six months after Ava was born. In addition, Ava's father had made millions at the firm. He was a shrewd investor and doubled his yearly earnings consistently. So when he died he left a pretty hefty estate, with enough to take care of his wife and daughter comfortably for the rest of their lives.

"I wanted my fairy tale," Eleanor continued. "I'd fallen madly in love with Haywood Cannon, and on our first date had pictured our lavish lives together. We would have a magnificent house full of beautiful children and want for absolutely nothing. I had to have an emergency hysterectomy after giving birth to you. Fifteen years later Haywood found out he was adopted. His birth brother killed four people before taking his own life. And when Haywood traced the rest of his family, he found out his parents were also criminals and had died in jail.

"He was devastated, and a glass of wine in the evenings turned into a bottle of scotch hidden in his office drawer, our bathroom and his home office. I thought if I continued on with our lives, proving to Haywood that I would stand by him no matter what his birthright, that things would eventually return to normal. The phone call in the middle of the night informing me that my husband was dead was a cruel wake-up call."

Eleanor blinked. Her eyes shone with tears. Ava couldn't speak—she didn't know what to say because she'd never heard this story before.

"Life happens, Ava. There's no way to plan for it, and no amount of running away from it will fix problems. It just happens."

"I could have told him," Ava said quietly and looked down at her hands. "I could have just told Gage the truth."

"And I could have insisted your father get help."

"It's not the same," Ava argued.

"The circumstances aren't, no. But the concept is. Look at me, Ava."

At the sharp tone, Ava's head shot up, and she stared back at her mother to see tears streaming down Eleanor's face.

"If I had told Haywood to get help, if I had insisted and then worked with him to get through the disillusionment he'd suffered, maybe he wouldn't have thought driving off that cliff was the only answer. I had the love of my life, and I didn't do enough to hold on to it."

When Ava opened her mouth to speak, her mother held up one elegant hand.

"If you had told Gage about the show for his family from day one, he might have said no and sent you away. Or he might have listened to you and let you speak to his family, and they might have all made a decision. But that time has passed. You cannot determine what the outcome would have been at this point any more than I can. But you still have the opportunity that I missed."

Ava shook her head. "I don't know what to do now. I mean, I do. I should just go. I betrayed him, all of them."

"You were doing your job and you fell in love. That's life. But you are no quitter," Eleanor told her. "You're not like me. Don't miss the opportunity to say something, do something, that might change the course of these events. If you really love this man, you need to grab hold of that love and don't let go."

She heard what her mother was saying, and she knew what she meant, but Ava was tired, and she was certain that she never wanted to see Gage looking at her the way he had just a short while ago again. Her heart couldn't take it.

"We're going home tomorrow, Mother," Ava said and crawled to the head of the bed to sit next to her mother. She took her hand and laid her head on Eleanor's shoulder. "Thank you for talking to me about Dad and what really happened. I'm sorry it didn't turn out better."

"Not as sorry as I am, my baby. Every day I wonder and I hurt. Well, every day until I met Otis."

That made Ava smile. "Wow. You and Otis."

Eleanor chuckled. "I know. There's just something about this town."

That was something else Ava and Eleanor could agree on. There was something about Temptation and the people here. Especially the Taylors. But that something would soon be in Ava's past. It had to be.

Chapter 14

Two weeks later

Gemma Taylor sat at the head of the formal dining room table in Gray's house. She was a tall woman, at five feet ten inches, with a heavily creamed coffee complexion and ink-black hair that fell in perfect soft waves past her shoulders. She sat with her shoulders squared, brown eyes searching and assessing everyone in the room with her. She looked, to Gage, just like their mother.

"This is ridiculous," Gage said. "There's nothing to discuss."

"That's not your call," Gemma told him calmly. "This involved all of us, so we should have all been consulted."

"I agree," Gray, who was sitting across the table from Gage, said. "This is how it should have happened from the start. All of us here, listening to what the network has to say and then deciding how to proceed."

"I don't want to be on a television show," Gage insisted.

"And neither do I," Garrek chimed in from the Skype call he'd been connected through. "But I don't think I can make that call for anyone else."

"He can't," Gia replied.

She and Gen had once again been connected to the meeting via FaceTime calls, with Harper and Morgan sitting at the table holding the phones.

"And you're certain Ava never mentioned this to you, Gage?" Gemma asked. "You could have simply dismissed it because you're so firm in your answer."

Gage stared at her blankly for a moment, and then he fumed. This was all Ava's fault. Now she was pitting them against each other.

"I definitely would have remembered her telling me that she was here to spy on my family for the sake of a new show," he said.

"It could have been after those steamy bouts of sex on your lovely yacht," Morgan said and then looked across the room as if she hadn't just aimed those words at him.

The doorbell rang, and Harper set her phone on the table, saying, "I'll get it."

Gage could have sworn he heard her chuckle as she walked out of the room and headed to the door. He wisely remained silent and sat back in the chair. He rested his hands on his thighs and decided to play this as cool as he possibly could. It wasn't going to be easy. Not like handing in his resignation to the hospital and packing up his condo had been. That was a surprise to him, because he'd spent his entire life striving to get to those places. It shouldn't have been so easy to walk away. But he hadn't wanted to examine the reasons for that. He'd just wanted to get back to Temptation and to get started on his new dream, even if a huge part of it had fallen through.

"Everyone, this is Ava Cannon. She's here on behalf of Donovan Network Television and would like to present a business opportunity to the family," Harper said.

Gage heard his siblings speaking to Ava and thanking her for coming. He did not turn around to look at her, nor did he say a word to her. He couldn't. There were no words to describe what these last two weeks had been like for him. And heaven help him, he couldn't figure out the words to make things better.

"Thank you for inviting me," Ava said.

From the sound of her voice, and because he could see her movement out of his peripheral vision, he could tell she'd entered the dining room and followed Harper to stand at the other end of the table.

"It's a pleasure to meet you all. I've heard a lot about you from…your family, and then I've done some research," Ava said.

"You should probably focus more on what the family says," Gemma joked. "Even though they can embellish a bit, too."

Everyone around the table laughed. Except Gage.

"Well, I'll get right to it," Ava said. She pulled out a laptop and placed it on the table. After tapping some keys, she turned it to face everyone.

Gage couldn't help but look. On the screen was a purple-and-gold logo that read The Taylors of Temptation. In seconds, that screen dissolved and in its place was Lemil Mountain Lake, the words "A Whole New World" appearing in shimmering letters over the water.

"Awww, it's the lake," Gia said. "You remember playing softball there, Gage? You were always begging Mom and Dad to take us there on pretty summer days."

"I hated swimming," Gen said. "But Gage loved the water."

"He still does," Gray said frankly.

Ava cleared her throat.

"I was first approached by producers at my former network to create a show surrounding the Taylors. It would have been a thirteen-episode reality show following each of you and your new life around Temptation. Marketing and scheduling were already in place. I didn't ask why in the beginning, but I should have. As it turns out, the producers had already worked out a deal for this show with Theodor Taylor. They'd even paid him an advance in the amount of seven million dollars."

Silence filled the room.

"I've since gathered additional information," Ava continued. "The advance money was wired to an account in the name of S. Frank Brewster. He was a carpenter who worked on the houses on Bond Street. S. Frank Brewster died last month, and his son, Tobias Brewster, has a Christmas tree farm just south of Temptation.

Tobias was kind enough to let me go through some of his father's papers, and I found email receipts of when Frank set up an account in Grand Cayman Island with 6.8 million dollars. The remaining money was reported as a fee to Frank from Theodor, and Tobias inherited it upon his father's death."

"I'll be damned," Gemma said, resting her elbows on the table and staring at the laptop screen.

"So Dad decided we were doing this show without conferring with us either," Gia said. "Ain't that something."

Gray shook his head. "It's something, all right."

Gage remained speechless. He'd said he didn't care about where the money had come from, but it was nice to finally hear about the money trail and receive the full story.

"When the executives came to me about the show, it was because upon Theodor's death, the signed contract they had became null and void. But they were out seven million dollars," Ava told them.

"So they needed you to come here and make it happen. They needed you to get the show on air because you'd done such a great job with *Doctor's Orders*," Morgan stated.

"And they knew that Gage had been working on the show with me," Ava said.

This time her voice—which Gage had been trying to convince himself he hadn't missed hearing—cracked a bit, and guilt settled into his chest like a pile of hot rocks.

"All of this was happening in LA," Harper said. "How did Millie find out?"

"I can explain that, too," Ava said. "My agent found out that Miranda Martinez, one of the actresses from *Doctor's Orders*, was sleeping with one of the execs at the network. She wanted to be involved in the reality show as a possible love interest."

Gage frowned at those words. He recalled Miranda's not-so-subtle advances when they'd been at the awards show.

Ava continued. "When they turned her down, Miranda threatened to leak the show idea to another network. To counter her threat, the execs hurried to release a preliminary announcement about the show to a few key press contacts. We assume someone from the press contacted Millie in the hopes of a background story about the town."

Gemma shook her head. "This is unbelievable," she said. "The things that go on in the world of television and celebrities."

Which was exactly why Gage had wanted nothing to do with this world. But hadn't he already been involved in the world? He was working on a television show, even as a consultant, and he'd been sleeping with a writer/producer.

"So what happens now?" Gen asked.

"I am no longer working with that network," Ava told them. "Their idea for the show and what I was willing to present to you were different. They weren't open to a compromise, and neither was I."

Gemma leaned over and pinched Gage's knee.

"Soon after I severed ties with the station, I went to Miami and met with Parker and Savian Donovan from Donovan Network Television. They asked about you, Gage," she said.

When all eyes fell on him, Gage looked down the table to Ava. She looked amazing in a black pantsuit and teal blouse. Her hair was pulled over to rest on one shoulder, and that spot he loved to kiss—the hollow of her neck—beckoned him. He cleared his throat.

"Why would they ask about me?"

"You met them when we were at the awards show, and they remembered," she replied.

"Oh, yeah. Right," Gage said, and after a pause continued. "What happened at the meeting?"

"I'm not sure if any of you have heard of them, but the Donovans are a very large and prestigious African American family. They have their hand in just about everything, from oil to television to casinos. Anyway, the Donovans are all about family first. So when Parker and Savian asked about Gage, I took that as a sign, and I pitched my revised idea for the Taylors of Temptation show. And they loved it!"

Gia squealed. "What's the revised idea?"

Ava explained the four-hour, two-night special and that they could decide which siblings appeared and how their story would be told. She talked about payment and contracts and negotiable points. She suggested, if they were considering it, that they should each get an agent or a lawyer to look over their contracts and advise them further of their rights before they commit.

And then she said, "I never meant to exploit any of

you, or what your parents went through. I was reluctant about even taking the job at first. But then I came to Temptation, and I saw Gray and Morgan and the kids. I met Harper and I listened to how she talked about Garrek and falling in love with him. I listened to Gage talk about your childhood and the things you lost because of the show. And I changed my mind. I didn't want to do anything that would hurt any of you. I should have told you all from the start, but I didn't know how."

She shook her head. "No. That's not true. I didn't want to. I didn't want my time with this family and with…" She paused, her gaze resting on Gage. "I didn't want any of it to end. So I pushed it off, and I worked on an idea that I thought would suit you better. But believe me, I understand completely if you don't want to take it. If you want to remain a family outside of the spotlight, I get it. I do, and I envy you for it."

"I'm in!" Gia yelled. "It'll be great exposure for my new restaurant."

"I think you're right," Gen added. "We could get some great advertising for our businesses out of this."

"I'm not sure what my schedule will be like," Garrek said. "But if you want to get in on the advertising possibilities, Harper, I'm okay with it."

Gage looked across the table to see Gray staring at him.

"Morgan and I have to talk about this," Gray said. "We're the only ones who have children involved, and I don't want to risk them in any way," he said.

Morgan reached out to take his hand. "We'll talk about it and figure out what works best for us."

Gemma smiled. "Well, I don't know. I've got a lot going on right now and…I just don't know."

Gage looked at his sister. He'd been wondering why she'd shown up in Temptation six weeks before their scheduled Christmas dinner, but he hadn't found a moment to ask her about it.

Conversation about the show and questions for Ava continued, but Gage didn't want to hear any of it. He'd heard enough and now…well, now he was right back to being unsure of what he should do or say. So he opted to leave instead.

He couldn't help it; he looked at Ava as he stood. She was in her element, talking about shows and episodes and advertising blocks. She was great at her job; that had never been a question to him. It was everything else. How she felt in his arms. How it felt to have her sleeping next to him, writhing beneath him, laughing beside him. All of that had been amazing and he'd fallen for it. Hard.

Now, he needed to figure out how to pick himself up again.

An hour later, Gage stepped out of the First Unity of Temptation Bank and looked up to the sky. That's where his mother was, and he wondered if she were looking down on him, curious as to what his next step would be. And if his father were in heaven, too, was he standing beside his wife—the woman Gage had once heard Theodor say was the love of his life—watching to see what their fifth-born child would do about his future at this moment?

Gage held the key his father had left for him in one hand, his cell phone in the other, and stood in the middle of the sidewalk on Crane Street for another few minutes. He looked up and down the street to the people moving about. The two male tourists who walked hand in hand looking into the window of a gift shop specializing in Lemil Mountain Lake memorabilia, and the grandfather across the street holding his young granddaughter's hand while they waited for the traffic light to change. Cars drove past, at a much slower speed than they traveled in New York, and the coffee shop just a few blocks down served coffee, sticky buns and much better conversation than the coffee place on the main level of Nancy Links Medical Center.

He smiled as he turned to walk toward where his car was parked, because in this moment Gage knew that he'd made the right decision. Although none of this had been part of his original plan, he felt with every fiber of his being that this was what his life was meant to be.

He drove for almost half an hour before parking his car on a grassy spot. He reached into his back pocket and pulled out the papers he'd retrieved from the safe-deposit box in the bank—the one that his special key had opened. He checked the address on the papers and then looked at his GPS. He had arrived at his destination, but there was nothing here.

Gage stepped out of the car and stuffed his keys into his pocket. He kept the papers in his hand, but rolled them up as he walked across the grass. There were acres of grass to one side, and to his delight, mountains on the other side. He continued to walk because he heard a familiar sound—the rustling of water over rocks and sand. The lake was about twenty miles ahead. Folding his arms over his chest, Gage stood and simply stared, enjoying the sight before him.

"Patsy and Jebediah Johnson built a house here sixty-two years ago," a woman said from behind.

Gage turned abruptly to see her standing there, wearing a long purple dress fringed in lace that looked as old as the years of which she'd spoken. Her gray hair was pulled up in a neat stack, pearl earrings at her ears that perfectly matched the color of the wool coat she wore. Her gloved hands were clasped in front of her while gray eyes stared directly at him.

"You don't remember me," she continued. "I'm JoEllen Camby, and I remember you very well. Patsy was beside herself with joy the moment she found out her daughter, Olivia, was pregnant. Teddy and Olivia had tried for so long, Jeb had begun to believe he'd never get grandchildren. But Patsy, oh, she was a praying woman. Yes indeed. She and I used to stay at the church long after Sunday service was over, and we'd go down to the altar and get on our knees. We prayed until times got better, yes, we did."

The woman talked with the old lyrical voice of someone who had seen and experienced a myriad of events, and nothing but her faith had brought her through. Her honey-brown skin was wrinkled and sagged a bit at the cheeks, but she stood straight and strong. She sounded wise and knowledgeable, and Gage was instantly captivated by her words.

"You and my grandmother prayed for the in vitro treatments to work," he stated.

"Yes, we sure did. Some silly folk in the church thought it wasn't godly, but we knew that the good Lord made a way for his faithful children. And if the only way Olivia and Teddy were going to have a baby was with the help of science, then so be it," Mrs. Camby said with a swift nod. "And, oh, when Teddy announced it at the town council meeting he was attending one night, we all cheered. We couldn't wait until the babies were born. Then those TV people came, and the devil went to work."

She shook her head then. "Olivia was unhappy after the first two years of the show. She wanted desperately to have her husband and her babies to herself. She cried to Patsy many a day, and Patsy walked up on my back porch or we came right out here to look at the water and talk about how such a happy time had gone sour so quickly. I thank the good Lord for taking Patsy and Jeb away from here in that fire, three years before their only daughter packed up her children and left town. But I still come out here from time to time."

Gage remembered his mother telling them about her parents and how they'd died. He also remembered talk of his great-grandfather, Patsy's father, who had offered his vacation home in Pensacola to Olivia and the children when she'd left. He'd lived until Gage and his siblings were fifteen.

"This is the land their house was on," he said after thinking on Mrs. Camby's words for a few seconds.

She nodded. "Yes. Right here. It was a great big ol'

house because Patsy had wanted more children, but that wasn't meant to be. The remnants of the house and the land fell to your mother after her parents died. So she could have repaired the house and moved you children here after what Teddy did to her. But I understand why she had to get away. Gossip can be unrelenting, especially in a town like Temptation."

"People have a hard time minding their own business," Gage said, thinking about Miranda and Millie.

"Ain't that the truth," Mrs. Camby said with a smile. "But this is your mother's land, free and clear."

Gage shook his head. "It's my land now," he said with a glib smile. "My mother apparently missed a tax payment at some point, and when the town would have foreclosed on it, my father bought it. And when he died," Gage said, holding up the hand with the rolled-up papers in it, "he left the land to me."

Mrs. Camby nodded and smiled. "Teddy loved himself some Olivia. I never believed he stopped loving her or his children."

"He just couldn't do right by her or us," Gage said drily.

"Every man can't make the right decision all the time. It's not natural," she told Gage. "You should know that for yourself. But if it's your land, you do with it as you please. Just don't forget the love that was here. That's what happens too many times to count—people forget about the love."

Gage didn't. He couldn't. And that's why he'd sent the text message to Ava before he'd left the bank.

For what seemed like a long stretch of time after Mrs.

Camby left him alone on the property, Gage heard a car stop and park. He looked out at the water, holding his breath and rehearsing the words in his head. He needed them to come out right, and he needed her to listen and to accept his apology, his heart and his soul.

Ava stepped out of the rental car and looked straight ahead to where Gage stood. His back was to her, but she had a feeling he knew she was there. Of course he should, since his text message had said for her to meet him here. She had only planned to stay in Temptation overnight, making herself available in case the Taylors had immediate questions about her offer. But she hadn't wanted to chance being here any longer because the memories were just too tough to ignore.

In the two weeks they'd been apart, Ava had used every ounce of strength she had to hold her head up and forge forward with her work. But there wasn't a moment in each day that she didn't think about him, about the brief time she'd been allowed the dream of what they could be together.

Seeing Gage earlier today had proven to her that the dream had fizzled and burned. He hadn't even wanted to look at her as she'd stood in his brother's house, and a part of her couldn't blame him. Another part was pissed with him for not at least hearing her out and then making an informed decision. And for not telling her about the woman who had broken his heart and his spirit. But that was beyond her control.

Walking toward him now was a bad idea—she sensed it, and yet she didn't pause.

"Thank you for coming," he said, when she finally stopped and stood silently beside him.

"You asked me to come because you had something to say. I wanted to give you the chance, even though you denied me the same," she said in a tone that she knew was frosty, but she couldn't help it.

He surprised her by replying, "I know. That's what I wanted to tell you, that I was an idiot."

"Oh," was all she could manage to say. "Well. Okay. Then I guess I'll get going."

Ava didn't know why exactly, but she hurriedly turned away to leave. Gage's hand on her arm stopped her.

"Don't," he said.

She glanced down to his hand and then up to him. He looked as good as she recalled. Not that it was logical to think that in fourteen days he would age fifty years, grow a potbelly and regret ever letting her go. That had been one of her thoughts when she was lying awake at night, cursing him for making her fall in love with him.

"Do you have something else to say?"

"I do," he told her. "But first, I've been thinking about this for the past two weeks."

"Thinking about wh—"

Her words were cut off when Gage pulled her to him, wrapping an arm tightly around her back to hold her there, and his lips crashed down over hers. The kiss was hot and rough, rugged and delicious. His tongue worked masterfully over hers, his hands moving over her back, down her arms and to cup her hips. She wrapped her arms around his neck because there was nothing else she'd rather do with them. Her palms flattened on the back of his head as she leaned into him and they took the kiss deeper.

"One perfect moment," Gage whispered when they finally broke apart.

He was breathing fast, and so was she.

"What?"

"This was the one perfect moment. Right here, in this place and at this time. It was the perfect moment to kiss you and to tell you that I'm madly in love with you. I want to spend the rest of my life with you," he said.

He was staring down at her so intently, and Ava was still trying to catch her breath. "Wait a minute. You told me to stay away from you and your family."

"And you didn't listen," he replied.

She nodded. "Yes. But you acted as if you wanted nothing else to do with me. And I kind of understood, because I lied."

"You should have trusted me enough to tell me what you were doing," he said.

She opened her mouth to speak again, but Gage kissed her once more. A slower kiss, but potent nonetheless.

"And I should have trusted you enough not to accuse you of being like Bethany. She's the woman I was involved with for two months, three years ago. I let her in and she lied and betrayed me. She killed my child, and while I get that it was her body and her decision, it was my child. I deserved to know."

"Yes," she said, her heart breaking at the memory of seeing him with Ryan, Emma, Jack and Lily. He was going to be a terrific father.

"You deserved to know," she continued.

"But you're nothing like her. And I should have trusted you enough to at least let you explain why you did what you did."

He took a breath and let it out quickly. "But it was easier and more familiar not to believe there was something good between us."

Ava sighed, because all the wind had been taken out of her sail. All the life that she'd thought she'd had in her had been washed away by this new feeling, this new opportunity for a life with Gage.

"I meant what I said, Gage. I never meant to hurt your or your family. I was just so focused on my work and proving myself to everyone. I love you and your family too much to ever intentionally hurt any of you," she said.

"Me," he said, lifting his fingers to run along the line of her jaw. "Right now, I just need you to say that you love me."

Her heart was thumping wildly in her chest. "I love you, Gage."

His smile and the warm hug that followed brought tears to her eyes as she thought about the fact that she never imagined she'd get to say those words to him.

"I want to build your tiny home right here in this spot so that when we're in Temptation we can look out at the lake, just like my grandparents used to do," he was saying.

Ava had pulled away from him and was now looking at him through eyes swimming in tears. "What did you just say?"

"We can set up a time to meet with Harper and her crew in the next few days, but I want to get started on the house relatively soon. And I want to marry you, Ava," Gage said.

"Wait, you're talking too fast and I can't keep up."

He chuckled. "Well, get out your notepad so you can take notes. I want to marry you. Not next year, but next month. All my family will be here for Christmas. What better time to start a new life with my beautiful new wife?"

"I don't know what to say," Ava managed as she used her hand to wipe away the tears.

Happy tears that she felt deep down in her soul. Tears that she shed for the love her parents had lost somewhere along the way, and for Theodor and Olivia Taylor, who had gotten swept away in the limelight and forfeited their love as a result. Between her and Gage, she felt all that love, all that hope, and wanted to reach out and grab it and hold on tight, just as her mother had advised.

"Say yes," he told her. "Say you'll marry me and we'll build this house and we'll live happily ever after, no matter what."

She was shaking her head as she cupped his face in her hands. "No matter what, Gage," she whispered. "I will love you and I will marry you and we will be happy together, no matter what."

* * * * *

#585 A STALLION DREAM
The Stallions • **by Deborah Fletcher Mello**
Collin Stallion plans to give back to the community by volunteering to exonerate someone wrongfully convicted of a crime. His partner in the high-profile case, powerhouse attorney London Jacobs, isn't impressed by the Stallion. Until passion ignites. But with adversaries looming, will they fulfill their dream of love?

#586 LOVE FOR ALL TIME
Sapphire Shores • **by Kianna Alexander**
Sapphire Shores is rolling out the red carpet for Sierra Dandridge—the "ice queen." But real estate scion Campbell Monroe finds nothing cold about the worldly beauty. Their desire culminates in an intimate affair. Until a younger actress's vicious social media campaign threatens Sierra's career and life...

#587 THE HEIRESS'S SECRET ROMANCE
The Kingsleys of Texas • **by Martha Kennerson**
Investigator Kathleen Winston's task is clear: uncover the truth about the alleged safety violations at Kingsley Oil and Gas. But one look at ruggedly sexy VP Morgan Kingsley and her scrutiny transforms into seduction! But can the emotionally guarded bachelor forgive Kathleen once her identity—and her heart—are revealed?

#588 WINNING HÉR FOREVER
Bay Point Confessions
by Harmony Evans
Construction entrepreneur Trent Waterson has a passion for hard work...and the one woman in Bay Point who tries to avoid him. Former dancer Sonya Young is stunned to learn that Trent's brother is scheming to buy her childhood home. Can Trent choose between family loyalty and their breathtaking chemistry?

KPCNM0818

SPECIAL EXCERPT FROM

HARLEQUIN

Collin Stallion plans to give back to the community by volunteering to exonerate someone wrongfully convicted of crime. His partner in the high-profile case—powerhouse attorney London Jacobs—isn't impressed by the seductive bachelor. Until passion ignites. But with an adversary threatening Collin's family legacy and London's ex-fiancé sworn to win her back, will they fulfill their dream of love?

Read on for a sneak peek at
A Stallion Dream,
the next exciting installment in
The Stallions series by Deborah Fletcher Mello!

Collin Stallion was sheer perfection, she thought as she stared in his direction. He'd changed into a casual suit of polished sateen. It was expertly tailored with clean, modern lines and fitted him exceptionally well. The color was a rich, deep burgundy and he wore a bright white T-shirt beneath it. He'd changed his shoes as well, a pair of pricey white Jordan sneakers now adorning his feet. He'd released his dreadlocks and the sun-kissed strands hung down his back past his broad shoulders. The thick tresses gave him a lionlike mane and he had the look of a regal emperor. He was too damn pretty and attracting a wealth of attention.

As their gazes locked and held, London felt her cheeks heat with color. Something she didn't recognize pulsed deep in her feminine core and the look he was giving her seemed to tease every ounce of her sensibilities. His eyes were intoxicating, their color a rich amber with flecks of gold that shimmered beneath the setting sun. There was something behind his stare that was heated, igniting a wealth of ardor in the pit of her stomach.

"Collin, hey!" she exclaimed as she reached his side. "I apologize. I didn't mean to be late. I hope you haven't been waiting here long."

He shook his head. "You're fine. You're right on time. I was actually early."

London nodded, suddenly feeling completely out of sorts. She was beyond nervous, her knees beginning to quiver ever so slightly. She felt him sense the rise of discomfort, his own anxiousness dancing sweetly with hers.

He took a deep breath. "Why don't we go inside. I'm sure our table is ready for us," he said as he pressed a gentle hand against the small of her back.

A jolt of electricity shot through London's body at his touch, the intensity of it feeling like she'd combusted from the inside out. It took everything in her not to trip across the threshold of the restaurant's front door.

Don't miss A Stallion Dream
*by Deborah Fletcher Mello, available September 2018
wherever Harlequin® Kimani Romance™
books and ebooks are sold.*